*Agatha Christie*

# And Then There Were None

## Agatha Christie

A SAMUEL FRENCH ACTING EDITION

**SAMUEL FRENCH**

FOUNDED 1830

SAMUELFRENCH.COM
SAMUELFRENCH-LONDON.CO.UK

ISBN 978-0-573-70231-0
www.SamuelFrench.com
www.SamuelFrench-London.co.uk

---

### FOR PRODUCTION ENQUIRIES

#### UNITED STATES AND CANADA
Info@SamuelFrench.com
1-866-598-8449

#### UNITED KINGDOM AND EUROPE
Theatre@SamuelFrench-London.co.uk
020-7255-4302

Each title is subject to availability from Samuel French, depending
upon country of performance. Please be aware that *AND THEN THERE
WERE NONE* may not be licensed by Samuel French in your territory.
Professional and amateur producers should contact the nearest Samuel
French office or licensing partner to verify availability.

---

## MUSIC USE NOTE

*AND THEN THERE WERE NONE* first opened at the Broadhurst Theatre in New York City on June 27, 1944. The performance was directed by Mr. DeCourville, with sets by Howard Bay. The cast was as follows:

**ROGERS** ........................................ Neil Fitzgerald

**MRS. ROGERS** .................................. Georgia Harvey

**FRED NARACOTT** .............................. Patrick O'Connor

**VERA CLAYTHORNE** ........................... Claudia Morgan

**PHILIP LOMBARD** ............................. Michael Whalen

**ANTHONY MARSTON** .................... Anthony Kemble Cooper

**WILLIAM BLORE** ............................... J. Pat O'Malley

**GENERAL MACKENZIE** .......................... Nicholas Joy

**EMILY BRENT** .................................. Estelle Winwood

**SIR LAWRENCE WARGRAVE** ..................... Halliwell Hobbes

**DR. ARMSTRONG** .............................. Harry Worth

# CHARACTERS

ROGERS

MRS. ROGERS

FRED NARRACOTT

VERA CLAYTHORNE

PHILIP LOMBARD

ANTHONY MARSTON

WILLIAM BLORE ~~GENERAL MACKENZIE~~ *Macarther*

EMILY BRENT

SIR LAWRENCE WARGRAVE

DR. ARMSTRONG

# SETTING

The living room of a house on Soldier Island, off the coast of Devon, England.

# TIME

ACT ONE
A summer evening in August.

ACT TWO
Scene I: The following morning.
Scene II: The same day-afternoon.

ACT THREE
Scene I: The same day-evening.
Scene II: The following afternoon.

# ACT ONE

*(The scene is the living room of the house on Soldier Island. It is a very modern room, and luxuriously furnished. It is a bright sunlight evening. Nearly the whole of the back of the stage is a window looking directly out to sea. French doors are open in center to balcony. It should give the impression of being like the deck of a liner almost overhanging the sea. There is a chair out right on the balcony and the main approach to the house is presumed to be up steps on the left side of the balcony. There is also presumed to be steps on the right of the balcony, but these are not the direct way up from the landing stage, but are supposed to lead around the house and up behind it, since the house is supposed to be built against the side of a steep hill. The French doors are wide so that a good area of the balcony is shown. In the left, near windows, is a door to dining room. Downstage left is a door communicating with hall. Pull cord below this door. Up right is a door to study. Middle stage right is fireplace. Over it hangs the reproduction of the "Ten Little Soldier Boys" nursery rhyme. On the mantelpiece is a group of ten china soldier boy figures. They are not spaced out, but clustered so that the exact number is not easily seen. The room is barely furnished with modern furniture, center are two sofas with space between. Chair and small table up left. Club chair with tabouret right and above it, down left, where there is also a bookcase. There is a window seat up right and cocktail cabinet below mantelpiece, tabouret down right. Before fireplace is a big white bearskin rug with a bear's head. There is an armchair and tabouret right center. A square ottoman at lower end of fireplace, a settee with table left of it in front of window right at back. When*

7

*curtain rises,* **ROGERS** *is busy putting final touches to room. He is setting out bottles down right.* **ROGERS** *is a competent middle-aged manservant. Not a butler, but a house-parlor man. Quick and deft. Just a trifle specious and shifty. There is a noise of seagulls. Motorboat horn heard off* **MRS. ROGERS** *enters from dining room up left. She is a thin, worried, frightened-looking woman. Enter* **NARRACOTT** *at center from left. He carries a market basket filled with packages.)*

**NARRACOTT**. First lot to be arriving in Jim's boat. Another lot not far behind. *(crosses left to her)*

**MRS. ROGERS**. Good evening, Fred.

**NARRACOTT**. Good evening, Mrs. Rogers.

**MRS. ROGERS**. Is that the boat?

**NARRACOTT**. Yes.

**MRS. ROGERS**. Oh, dear, already? Have you remembered everything?

**NARRACOTT**. *(giving her basket)* I think so. Lemons. Slip soles. Cream. Eggs, tomatoes and butter. That's all, wasn't it?

**MRS. ROGERS**. That's right. So much to do I don't know where to start. No maids till the morning, and all these guests arriving today.

**ROGERS**. *(at mantel)* Calm down, Ethel, everything's shipshape now. Looks nice, don't it, Fred?

**NARRACOTT**. Looks neat enough for me. Kind of bare, but rich folks like places bare, it seems.

**MRS. ROGERS**. Rich folks is queer.

**NARRACOTT**. And he was a queer sort of gentleman as built this place. Spent a wicked lot of money on it he did, and then gets tired of it and puts the whole thing up for sale.

**MRS. ROGERS**. Beats me why the Owens wanted to buy it, living on a island.

**ROGERS**. Oh, come off it, Ethel, and take all that stuff out into the kitchen. They'll be here any minute now.

*Scean not in book*

**MRS. ROGERS.** Making that steep climb an excuse for a drink, I suppose. Like some others I know.

*(motorboat horn heard off)*

**NARRACOTT.** That be young Jim. I'll be getting along. There's two gentlemen arriving by car, I understand. *(goes up to balcony)*

**MRS. ROGERS.** *(calling to him)* I shall want at least five loaves in the morning and eight pints of milk, remember.

**NARRACOTT.** Right.

*(***MRS. ROGERS*** *puts basket on the floor up left; exits to hall left 1.)*

**ROGERS.** *(breaks to right of window)* Don't forget the oil for the engine, Fred. I ought to charge up tomorrow, or I'll have the lights running down.

**NARRACOTT.** *(going off at left)* 'Twas held up on railway. It's at the station now. I'll bring it across the first thing tomorrow.

**ROGERS.** And give a hand with the luggage, will you?

**NARRACOTT.** Right.

**MRS. ROGERS.** *(enters with list)* I forgot to give you the list of guests, Tom.

**ROGERS.** Thanks, old girl. *(looks reflectively at list)* H'mm, doesn't look a very classy lot to me. *(refers to list)* Miss Claythorne. She'll probably be the secretary.

**MRS. ROGERS.** I don't hold much with secretaries. Worse than hospital nurses, and them giving themselves airs and graces and looking down on the servants.

**ROGERS.** Oh, stop grousing, Ethel, and cut along to that lovely up-to-date expensive kitchen of yours.

**MRS. ROGERS.** *(picks up basket; going out left 2)* Too many new-fangled gadgets for my fancy!

*(Voices of* **VERA** *and* **LOMBARD** *heard outside.* **ROGERS** *stands at center doors ready to receive them. He is now the well-trained, deferential manservant.* **VERA** *and* **LOMBARD** *enter from left on balcony. She is a*

*Story behind
house is different*

*good-looking girl of twenty-five. He is an attractive,
lean man of thirty-four, well-tanned, with a touch of the
adventurer about him. He is already a good deal taken
with* **VERA.***)*

**LOMBARD.** *(gazing round room, very interested)* So this is it!

**VERA.** How perfectly lovely!

**ROGERS.** Miss Claythorne!

**VERA.** You're – Rogers?

**ROGERS.** Yes. Good evening, Miss.

**VERA.** Good evening, Rogers. Will you bring up my luggage
and Captain Lombard's?

**ROGERS.** Very good, Miss. *(He exits through center windows to
left.)*

**VERA.** *(to* **LOMBARD,** *coming right center into room)* You've
been here before?

**LOMBARD.** No – but I've heard a lot about the place.

**VERA.** From Mr. and Mrs. Owen?

**LOMBARD.** *(crossing down left)* No, old Johnny Brewer, a pal
of mine, built this house – it's a sad and poignant story.

**VERA.** A love story?

**LOMBARD.** Yes, ma'am – the saddest of all. He was a wealthy
old boy and fell in love with the famous Lily Logan –
married her – bought the island and built this place
for her.

**VERA.** Sounds most romantic.

**LOMBARD.** Poor Johnny! He thought by cutting her off
from the rest of the world – without even a telephone
as means of communication – he could hold her.

**VERA.** But of course the fair Lily tired of her ivory tower –
and escaped?

**LOMBARD.** U'huh. Johnny went back to Wall Street, made a
few more millions, and the place was sold.

**VERA.** And here we are. *(moving as if to go out of door left 1)*
Well, I ought to find Mrs. Owen. The others will be up
in a minute.

**LOMBARD.** *(stopping her)* It would be very rude to leave me here all by myself.

**VERA.** Would it? Oh, well, I wonder where she is?

**LOMBARD.** She'll come along when she's ready. While we're waiting, *(nodding toward cabinet down right)* do you think I could have a drink? I'm very dry. *(goes below sofa to down right and starts preparing drinks)*

**VERA.** Of course you could.

**LOMBARD.** It's certainly warm after that steep climb. What's yours?

**VERA.** No, thanks, not for me – not on duty. *(to behind chair, right center)*

**LOMBARD.** A good secretary is never off duty.

**VERA.** Really. *(looking round room)* This is exciting! *(goes below sofa to up center)*

**LOMBARD.** What?

**VERA.** All this. The smell of the sea – the gulls – the beach and this lovely house. I am going to enjoy myself.

**LOMBARD.** *(smiling, coming to her)* I think you are. I think we both are. *(holding up drink)* Here's to you – you're very lovely.

*(**ROGERS** enters center from left with two suitcases and comes down left center.)*

**VERA.** *(to **ROGERS**)* Where is Mrs. Owen?

**ROGERS.** Mr. and Mrs. Owen won't be down from London until tomorrow, Miss. I thought you knew.

**VERA.** Tomorrow – but –

**ROGERS.** I've got a list here of the guests expected, Miss, if you would like to have it. The second boatload's just arriving. *(holds out list)*

**VERA.** Thank you.

*(takes list, **ROGERS** goes into hall left 1)*

How awful – I say, you will be sweet and help me, won't you?

**LOMBARD.** I won't move from your side.

**VERA**. Thank you.

*(She reads list. They both move down right.)*

It seems silly to have brought only us in the first boat and all the rest in the second.

**LOMBARD**. That, I'm afraid, was design, not accident.

**VERA**. Design? What do you mean?

**LOMBARD**. I suggested to the boatman that there was no need to wait for any more passengers. That and five shillings soon started up the engine.

**VERA**. *(laughing)* Oh, you shouldn't have done that!

**LOMBARD**. Well, they're not a very exciting lot, are they?

**VERA**. I thought the young man was rather nice-looking.

**LOMBARD**. Callow. Definitely callow. And very, very young.

**VERA**. I suppose you think a man in his thirties is more attractive.

**LOMBARD**. I don't think, my darling – I know.

*(**MARSTON** enters center from left. A good-looking young man of twenty-three or so, rich, spoiled – not very intelligent.)*

**MARSTON**. *(coming down right to them)* Wizard place you've got here.

*(**MARSTON** prepares to greet **VERA** as his hostess; **LOMBARD** stands beside her like a host)*

**VERA**. *(shakes hands)* I'm Mrs. Owen's secretary. Mrs. Owen has been detained in London, I'm afraid, and won't be down until tomorrow.

**MARSTON**. *(vaguely)* Oh, too bad.

**VERA**. May I introduce Captain Lombard, Mr. – er –

**MARSTON**. Marston, Anthony Marston.

**LOMBARD**. Have a drink?

**MARSTON**. Oh, thank you.

*(**BLORE** comes up on balcony from left. A middle-aged, thickset man; is wearing rather loud clothes and is*

*giving his impression of a gold magnate. His eyes dart about, making notes of everything.)*

**LOMBARD.** What will you have? Gin, whiskey, sherry – ?

**MARSTON.** Whiskey, I think.

*(They go down right to cabinet.)*

**BLORE.** *(Comes down right to* **VERA** *at right center. Seizing* **VERA***'s hand and wringing it heartily.)* Wonderful place you have here.

**VERA.** I'm Mrs. Owen's secretary. Mrs. Owen has been detained in London, I'm afraid, and won't be down until tomorrow.

**LOMBARD.** Say when!

**MARSTON.** Oh, wizard!

**BLORE.** How are you? *(makes for cocktail cabinet)*

**LOMBARD.** My name's Lombard. Have a drink, Mr. –

**BLORE.** Davis. Davis is the name.

**LOMBARD.** Mr. Davis – Mr. Marston!

*(***VERA** *sits on right sofa)*

**BLORE.** How are you, Mr. Marston? Pleased to meet you. Thanks, Mr. Lombard. I don't mind if I do. Bit of a stiff climb up here. *(he goes up center to balcony)* But whew! What a view and what a height! Reminds me of South Africa, this place. *(comes down center)*

**LOMBARD.** *(staring at him)* Does it? What part?

**BLORE.** Oh – er – Natal, Durban, you know.

**LOMBARD.** *(crosses center)* Really? *(hands him drink)*

**BLORE.** Well, here's to temperance. Do you – er – know South Africa?

**LOMBARD.** Me? No.

**BLORE.** *(with renewed confidence)* That's where I come from. That's my Natal state – ha ha.

**LOMBARD.** Interesting country. I should think.

**BLORE.** Finest country in the world, sir. Gold, silver, diamonds, oranges, everything a man could want. Talk about a land flowing with beer and skittles. *(goes to cocktail cabinet down right)*

*(***GENERAL MACKENZIE*** *arrives on balcony from left; upright soldierly old man with a gentle, tired face.)*

**MACKENZIE.** *(hesitating courteously.)* Er – How do you do?

*(***VERA*** *rises; meets him above sofa seat)*

**VERA.** General MacKenzie, isn't it? I'm Mrs. Owen's secretary. Mrs. Owen has been detained in London, I'm afraid, and won't be down until tomorrow. Can I introduce Captain Lombard – Mr. Marston and Mr. –

*(***MACKENZIE*** *crosses toward them.)*

**BLORE.** *(approaching him)* Davis, Davis is the name. *(shakes hands)*

**LOMBARD.** Whiskey and soda, sir?

**MACKENZIE.** Er – thanks. *(goes down right; studies ***LOMBARD***)* You in the service?

**LOMBARD.** Formerly in the King's African Rifles. Too tame for me in peace time. I chucked it.

**MACKENZIE.** Pity.

*(as ***LOMBARD*** *pours out soda)*

When.

*(***MISS EMILY BRENT*** *arrives center from left. She is a tall, thin spinster with a disagreeable, suspicious face.)*

**EMILY.** *(sharply to ***VERA***)* Where is Mrs. Owen? *(puts case on left sofa)*  confused

**VERA.** Miss Brent, isn't it? I'm Mrs. Owen's secretary. Mrs. Owen has been detained in London, I'm afraid.

*(***LOMBARD*** *to right of* ***EMILY***)*

**LOMBARD & VERA.** And won't be down until tomorrow.

*(They trail off, rather embarrassed.)*

**EMILY.** Indeed. Extraordinary. Did she miss the train?

**VERA**. I expect so. Won't you have something? May I introduce Captain Lombard – General MacKenzie – Mr. Marston. I think you all met on the boat. And Mr. –

**BLORE**. Davis, Davis is the name. May I take your case? *(up to **EMILY**, then goes behind her to right)*

**LOMBARD**. Do let me give you a drink? A dry martini? A glass of sherry? Whiskey and soda?

**EMILY**. *(coldly)* I never touch alcohol.

**LOMBARD**. You never touched alcohol!

**EMILY**. *(She picks up the case; goes below sofa to left.)* I suppose you know, young man, that you left us standing there on the wharf?

**VERA** I'm afraid, Miss Brent, I was to blame for that. I wanted to –

**EMILY**. It seems to me most extraordinary that Mrs. Owen should not be here to receive her guests.

**VERA** *(smiling)* Perhaps she's the kind of person who just can't help missing trains.

**BLORE**. *(laughs)* That's what I reckon she is.

**EMILY**. Not at all. Mrs. Owen isn't the least like that.

**LOMBARD**. *(lightly)* Perhaps it was her husband's fault.

**EMILY**. *(sharply)* She hasn't got a husband.

*(**VERA** stares. Enter **ROGERS** left 2.)*

I should like to go to my room.

**VERA**. Of course. I'll take you there.

**ROGERS**. *(to **VERA**)* You'll find Mrs. Rogers upstairs, Miss. She will show you the room.

*(exit **VERA** and **EMILY** left 1, **ROGERS** exits left 1, **WARGRAVE** enters center from left; comes center)*

**LOMBARD**. *(comes forward)* I'm afraid our host and hostess haven't arrived, sir. My name's Lombard.

**WARGRAVE**. Mine's Wargrave. How do you do?

**LOMBARD**. How do you do? Have a drink, sir?

**WARGRAVE**. Yes, please. A whiskey.

**BLORE**. *(crosses to* **WARGRAVE***)* How are you? Davis, Davis is the name.

*(***LOMBARD** *gets his drink; affably to* **WARGRAVE:***)*

I say, wonderful place you've got here. Quite unique.

**WARGRAVE**. As you say – quite unique.

**BLORE**. Your drink, sir.

*(***WARGRAVE** *puts coat on sofa left, takes his drink and sits up left, watches proceedings from there.)*

**MARSTON**. *(to* **LOMBARD***)* Old Badger Berkely rolled up yet?

**LOMBARD**. Who did you say?

**MARSTON**. Badger Berkely. He roped me in for this show. When's he coming?

**LOMBARD**. I don't think he is coming. Nobody of the name of Berkely.

**MARSTON**. *(jaw drops)* The dirty old double-crosser! He's let me down. Well, it's a pretty wizard island. Rather a wizard girl, that secretary. She ought to liven things up a bit. I say, old man, what about dressing for dinner if there's time?

**LOMBARD**. Let's go and explore.

**MARSTON**. How wizard!

**LOMBARD**. Things are a bit at sixes and sevens with the Owens not turning up.

**MARSTON**. Tricky, what? I say, wizard place for a holiday, what?

*(Exit* **MARSTON** *and* **LOMBARD** *left 1.* **BLORE** *wanders out on balcony, looks back sharply into room, and presently exits right on balcony as* **GENERAL MACKENZIE** *and* **WARGRAVE** *talk.* **WARGRAVE** *continues to sit like a Buddha. He observes* **MACKENZIE**, *who is right center, standing looking rather lost, absentmindedly pulling his moustache.* **MACKENZIE** *is carrying a shooting stick. He looks at it wistfully, half opens and closes it.)*

**WARGRAVE**. Aren't you going to sit down?

MACKENZIE. Well, to tell you the truth, you seem to be in my chair.

WARGRAVE. I am sorry. I didn't realize you were one of the family.

MACKENZIE. Well, it's not that exactly. To tell you the truth, I've never been here before. But you see I live at the Benton Club – have for the last ten years. And my seat is just about there. Can't get used to sitting anywhere else.

WARGRAVE. It becomes a bit of a habit. *(he rises; breaks to right)*

MACKENZIE. Yes, it certainly does. Thank you – *(sits up left)* Well, it's not quite as good as the Club's, but it's a nice chair. *(confidentially)* To tell you the truth. I was a bit surprised when I got this invitation. Haven't had anything of the kind for well over four years. Very nice of them, I thought.

ROGERS. *(enters left 1, picks up WARGRAVE's coat from sofa)* Can I have your keys, sir?

WARGRAVE. Is Lady Constance Culmington expected here, can you tell me? *(gives him keys)*

ROGERS. *(surprised)* Lady Constance Culmington? I don't think so, sir. Unless she's coming down with Mr. and Mrs. Owen.

WARGRAVE. Oh.

ROGERS. Allow me, sir. *(takes MACKENZIE's coat)* Can I have your keys, sir?

MACKENZLE. *(rising, crossing down left)* No, thanks. I'll unpack for myself.

ROGERS. Dinner is at eight o'clock, sir. Shall I show you to your room?

MACKENZIE. Please.

*(MACKENZIE goes to door left 1, which ROGERS holds open for him. WARGRAVE follows more deliberately, looking around room in an unsatisfied fashion. ROGERS follows them out. Sound of seagulls, then DR.*

ARMSTRONG *arrives upon balcony from left, followed by* NARRACOTT *carrying his suitcase.* ARMSTRONG *is a fussy, good-looking man of forty-four. He looks rather tired.)* ᶦn his 30s in book

NARRACOTT. Here you are, sir. I'll call Rogers. *(exits left 1)*

(ARMSTRONG *looks round, nods approval, looks out at sea. Then* NARRACOTT *returns.* ARMSTRONG *tips him.* NARRACOTT *exits to center left.* ARMSTRONG *sits settee up right.* BLORE *comes along balcony from right; pauses at sight of* ARMSTRONG.*)*

BLORE. *(to above settee)* How are you? Davis. Davis is the name.

ARMSTRONG. Mine's Armstrong. *(rises)*

BLORE. Doctor Armstrong, I believe.

ARMSTRONG. Yes.

BLORE. Thought so. Never forget a face.

ARMSTRONG. Don't tell me I've forgotten one of my patients!

BLORE. No, no, nothing like that, but I once saw you in Court giving expert evidence.

ARMSTRONG. Oh, really? Are you interested in the law?

BLORE. Well, you see, I'm from South Africa. Naturally, legal processes in this country are bound to interest a colonial.

ARMSTRONG. Oh, yes, of course.

BLORE. *(crossing down right)* Have a drink?

ARMSTRONG. No, thanks. I never touch it.

BLORE. Do you mind if I do? Mine's empty.

ARMSTRONG. Not a bit.

BLORE. *(pours himself a drink)* I've been having a look round the island. It's a wonderful place, isn't it?

ARMSTRONG. *(crossing to center)* Wonderful. I thought as I was coming across the mainland what a haven of peace this was.

**BLORE.** *(up to him, putting his face close to his)* Too peaceful for some, I daresay.

**ARMSTRONG.** *(moves to left)* Wonderfully restful. Wonderful for the nerves. I'm a nerve specialist, you know.

**BLORE.** Yes, I know that. Did you come down by train? *(goes to him)*

**ARMSTRONG.** *(up left to window)* No, I motored down. Dropped in on a patient on the way. Great improvement – wonderful response.

**BLORE.** *(up to him)* Best part of two hundred miles, isn't it? How long did it take you?

**ARMSTRONG.** *(to up right center)* I didn't hurry. I never hurry. Bad for the nerves. Some mannerless young fellow nearly drove me into the ditch near Amesbury. Shot past me at about eighty miles an hour. Disgraceful bit of driving. I'd like to have had his number.

**BLORE.** *(comes to him)* Yes, and if only more people would take the numbers of these young road hogs.

**ARMSTRONG.** Yes. You must excuse me. I must have a word with Mr. Owen. *(he bustles out left 1)*

**BLORE.** *(following down left)* Oh, but – Mr. Owen isn't coming down –

*(BLORE rings bell below left 1 door, finishes drink, puts glass on left sofa. ROGERS enters almost immediately, left 1.)*

**ROGERS.** You rang, sir?

**BLORE.** Yes, take my hat, will you? *(hands him his cap)* What time's supper?

**ROGERS.** Dinner is at eight o'clock, sir. *(pauses)* In a quarter of an hour. I think tonight dressing will be optional.

**BLORE.** *(familiarly)* Got a good place, here.

**ROGERS.** *(draws himself up rather stiffly)* Yes, thank you, sir.

**BLORE.** Been here long?

**ROGERS.** Just under a week, sir.

**BLORE.** Is that all? *(pause)* So I don't suppose you know much about this crowd that's here?

**ROGERS.** No, sir.

**BLORE.** All old friends of the family?

**ROGERS.** I really couldn't say, sir.

**BLORE.** Oh, well – Oh, Rogers –

**ROGERS.** Yes, sir?

**BLORE.** Rogers, do you think you could put some sandwiches and a bottle of beer in my room at night? I get an 'el of an appetite with this sea air.

**ROGERS.** I'll see what I can do, sir.

**BLORE.** Rogers – I'll see you won't lose by it. Where's my room?

**ROGERS.** I'll show you, sir.

**BLORE.** *(as they go out)* Good, I can do with a wash and brush up straightaway.

*(exits left 1 with* **ROGERS***)*

*(Enter* **MRS. ROGERS** *left 2. She picks up glass from sofa and from table up left and takes them down right, enter* **ROGERS** *with tray of eight glasses.)*

**MRS. ROGERS.** *(She takes glasses off tray and* **ROGERS** *puts on dirty ones.)* Oh, there you are, Rogers. You ought to clear these dirty glasses. You're always leaving the dirty work to me. Here I am with a four-course dinner on my hands and no one to help me. You might come and give me a hand with the dishing up. *(to above left sofa)* Who was it that you were talking to, by the way?

**ROGERS.** Davis. South African gentleman. No class if you ask me – and no money either.

**MRS. ROGERS.** *(comes down right of sofa to center)* I don't like him – Don't like any of 'em much. More like that bunch we had in the boarding house, I'd say.

**ROGERS.** Davis gives out he's a millionaire or something. You should see his underwear! Cheap as they make 'em.

**MRS. ROGERS**. Well, as I said, it's not treating us right. All these visitors arriving today and the maids not coming till tomorrow. What do they think we are?

**ROGERS**. Now, then – Anyway, the money's good.

**MRS. ROGERS**. So it ought to be! Catch me going into service again unless the money was good.

**ROGERS**. *(to center)* Well, it is good, so what are you going on about?

**MRS. ROGERS**. Well, I can tell you this, Rogers. I'm not staying any place where I'm put upon. Cooking's my business! I'm a good cook –

**ROGERS**. *(placating her)* First rate, old girl.

**MRS. ROGERS**. But the kitchen's my place and housework's none of my business. All these guests! I've a good mind to put my hat and coat on and walk out now and go straight back to Plymouth.

**ROGERS**. *(grinning)* You can't do that, old girl,

**MRS. ROGERS**. *(belligerently)* Who says I can't? Why not, I should like to know?

**ROGERS**. Because you're on a island, old girl. Had you forgotten that?

**MRS. ROGERS**. Yes, and I don't know as I fancy being on an island.

**ROGERS**. Don't know that I do, either, come to that. No slipping down to a pub, or going to the pictures. Oh, well, it's double wages on account of the difficulties. And there's plenty of beer in the house. *drinking*

**MRS. ROGERS**. That's all you ever think about – beer. *Problem*

**ROGERS**. Now, now, stop your nagging. You get back to the kitchen or your dinner will be spoilt.

**MRS. ROGERS**. It'll be spoilt anyway, I expect. Everybody's going to be late. Wasted on them, anyway. Thank goodness, I didn't make a souffle.

*(Enter* **VERA** *left 1,* **MRS. ROGERS** *goes to left 2 door.)*

Oh, dinner won't be a minute, Miss. Just a question of dishing up. *(exits left 2)*

*Betrice Taylor*

**VERA.** *(to above left sofa)* Is everything all right, Rogers? Can you manage between the two of you?

**ROGERS.** *(crossing, up left)* Yes, thank you, Miss. The Missus talks a lot, but she gets it done. *(exits left 2)*

*(VERA goes to right window. EMILY enters left 1, having changed.)*

**VERA.** What a lovely evening!

**EMILY.** Yes, indeed. The weather seems very settled. *(to center window)*

**VERA.** *(comes down right)* How plainly one can hear the sea.

**EMILY.** A pleasant sound. *(comes down center)*

**VERA.** Hardly a breath of wind – and deliciously warm. Not like England at all.

**EMILY.** I should have thought you might feel a little uncomfortable in that dress.

**VERA.** *(not taking the point)* Oh, no.

**EMILY.** *(nastily)* It's rather tight, isn't it?

**VERA.** *(good-humored)* Oh, I don't think so.

**EMILY.** *(sits left sofa; takes out gray knitting)* You'll excuse me, my dear, but you're a young girl and you've got your living to earn.

**VERA.** Yes?

**EMILY.** A well-bred woman doesn't like her secretary to appear flashy. It looks, you know, as though you were trying to attract the attention of the opposite sex.

**VERA.** *(coming to right center)* And would you say I do attract them?

**EMILY.** That's beside the point. A girl who deliberately sets out to get the attention of men won't be likely to keep her job long.

**VERA.** *(laughing at her)* Ah! Surely that depends on who she's working for?

**EMILY.** Really, Miss Claythorne!

**VERA.** Aren't you being a little unkind?

*Vera fighting with emily*

EMILY. *(spitefully)* Young people nowadays behave in the most disgusting fashion.

VERA. Disgusting?

EMILY. *(carried away)* Yes. Low-backed evening dresses. Lying half naked on beaches. All this so-called sunbathing. An excuse for immodest conduct, nothing more. Familiarity! Christian names – drinking cocktails! And look at the young men nowadays. Decadent! Look at that young Marston. What good is he? And that Captain Lombard!

VERA. What do you object to in Captain Lombard? I should say he was a man who'd led a very varied and interesting life.

EMILY. The man's an adventurer. All this younger generation is no good – no good at all.

VERA. *(breaks to right)* You don't like youth – I see.

EMILY. *(sharply)* What do you mean?

VERA. I was just remarking that you don't like young people.

EMILY. *(rises; moves up left)* And is there any reason why I should, pray?

VERA. Oh, no – *(pauses)* but it seems to me that you must miss an awful lot.

EMILY. You're very impertinent.

VERA. *(quietly)* I'm sorry, but that's just what I think.

EMILY. The world will never improve until we stamp out immodesty.

VERA. *(to herself)* Quite pathological. *(goes down right)*

EMILY. *(sharply)* What did you say?

VERA. Nothing.

(EMILY *sits up left. Enter* ARMSTRONG *and* LOMBARD *left 1, talking. They cross up right.*)

LOMBARD. What about the old boy –

ARMSTRONG. He looks rather like a tortoise, don't you think so?

**LOMBARD**. All judges look like tortoises. They have that venomous way of darting their heads in and out. Mr. Justice Wargrave is no exception.

**ARMSTRONG**. I hadn't realized he was a judge.

**LOMBARD**. Oh, yes. *(cheerfully)* He's probably been responsible for sending more innocent people to their death than anyone in England.

different

*(WARGRAVE enters and looks at him.)*

Hello, you. *(to VERA)* Do you two know each other? Mr. Armstrong – Miss Claythorne. Armstrong and I have just decided that the old boy –

**VERA**. Yes, I heard you and so did he, I think.

*(WARGRAVE moves over to EMILY. EMILY rises as she sees WARGRAVE approaching.)*

**EMILY**. Oh, Sir Lawrence.

**WARGRAVE**. Miss Brent, isn't it?

**EMILY**. There's something I want to ask you. *(EMILY indicating she wants to talk to him on the balcony)* Will you come out here?

**WARGRAVE**. *(as they go)* A remarkably fine night!

*(They go out center.)*

*(LOMBARD up center, MARSTON enters left 1 with BLORE, they are in conversation.)*

**MARSTON**. Absolutely wizard car – a super-charged Sports Varletti Carlotta. You don't see many of them on the road. I can get over a hundred out of her.

*(VERA sits on right sofa.)*

**BLORE**. Did you come from London?

**MARSTON**. Yes, two hundred and eight miles and I did it in a bit over four hours.

*(ARMSTRONG turns and looks at him.)*

Too many cars on the road, though, to keep it up. Touched ninety going over Salisbury Plain. Not too bad, eh?

ARMSTRONG. I think you passed me on the road.

MARSTON. Oh, yes?

ARMSTRONG. You nearly drove me into the ditch.

MARSTON. *(unmoved)* Did I? Sorry. *(to above left sofa)*

ARMSTRONG. If I'd seen your number, I'd have reported you.

MARSTON. But you were footling along in the middle of the road.

ARMSTRONG. Footling? Me footling?

BLORE. *(to relieve atmosphere)* Oh, well, what about a drink?

MARSTON. Good idea.

*(They move toward the drinks down right.)*

Will you have one, Miss Claythorne?

*(LOMBARD drops down toward VERA.)*

VERA. No, thank you.

LOMBARD. *(sitting beside VERA on sofa)* Good evening, Mrs. Owen.

VERA. Why Mrs. Owen?

LOMBARD. You'd make the most attractive wife for any wealthy businessman.

VERA. Do you always flirt so outrageously?

LOMBARD. Always.

VERA. Oh! Well, now we know. *(She turns half away, smiling.)*

LOMBARD. Tell me, what's old Miss Brent talking to the Judge about? She tried to buttonhole him upstairs.

VERA. I don't know. Funny – she seemed so definite that there wasn't a Mr. Owen.

LOMBARD. You don't think that Mrs. Owen – I mean that there isn't – that they aren't –

VERA. What, married you mean?

*(ROGERS enters left 2, switches on lights, draws curtains and exits to study up right. MARSTON comes to right end of left sofa. LOMBARD rises to left end sofa.)*

MARSTON. Damn shame we don't know each other. I could have given you a lift down.

VERA. Yes, that would have been grand.

MARSTON. Like to show you what I can do across Salisbury Plain. Tell you what – maybe we can drive back together?

*(Enter* WARGRAVE *and* EMILY *center,* MACKENZIE *enters; sits chair down left.)*

VERA. *(surprised)* But I – *(rising)*

MARSTON. But it seems damn silly. I've got an empty car.

LOMBARD. Yes, but she likes the way she's going back and –

VERA. *(crosses to fireplace)* Look! Aren't they sweet? Those ten little china soldiers.

(MARSTON *and* LOMBARD *scowl at each other.)* *[handwritten: fighting for vera]*

Oh, and there's the old nursery rhyme.

LOMBARD. What are you talking about? What figures? What nursery rhyme?

VERA. *(She points at the figures and rhyme-reading:)* "Ten little soldier boys going out to dine.
One choked his little self and then there were nine – "

*(ROGERS *enters up right and crosses left.* VERA *continues reading nursery rhyme,* BLORE *crosses up to below her;* EMILY *to above her.)*

"Nine little soldier boys sat up very late.
One overslept himself and then there were eight."
*(crosses left)*

BLORE. "Eight little soldier boys traveling in Devon.
One got left behind and then there were seven – "

VOICE. *(very slowly and clearly from off up right)* Ladies and Gentlemen, silence, please!

*(All rise. Everybody stops talking and stares round at each other, at the walls. As each name is mentioned that person reacts by a sudden movement or gesture.)*

You are charged with these indictments: that you did respectively and at diverse times commit the following: Edward Armstrong, that you did cause the death of Louisa Mary Clees. William Henry Blore, that you brought about the death of James Stephen Lendor. Emily Caroline Brent, that you were responsible for the death of Beatrice Taylor. Vera Elizabeth Claythorne, that you killed Peter Ogilvie Hamilton. Cyril

*(VERA sits on left sofa.)*

Philip Lombard, that you were guilty of the deaths of twenty-one men, members of an East African tribe. John Gordon MacKenzie, that you sent your wife's lover, Arthur Richmond, to his death.

*(MACKENZIE sits down left.)*

Anthony James Marston, that you were guilty of the murder of John and Lucy Combes. Thomas Rogers and Ethel Rogers, that you brought about the death of Jennifer Brady. Lawrence John Wargrave, that you were guilty of the murder of Edward Seton. Prisoners at the bar, have you anything to say in your defense?

*(There is a momentary paralyzed silence, then there is a scream outside the door left 2. LOMBARD springs across the room to it. Indignant murmur breaks out as people recover from the first shock. Door left 2 opens to show MRS. ROGERS in a fallen heap. MARSTON springs across to LOMBARD. They pick up MRS. ROGERS and carry her in to right sofa. ARMSTRONG comes to her.)*

ARMSTRONG. It's nothing much. She's fainted, that's all. She'll be round in a minute. Get some brandy

BLORE. Rogers, get some brandy.

*(ROGERS, shaking all over, goes out left 2.)*

VERA. Who was that speaking? It sounded –

MACKENZIE. *(above left sofa, hands shaking, pulling at his moustache)* What's going on here? What kind of practical joke was that?

*(BLORE wipes face with handkerchief, **WARGRAVE** stands in middle of room near sofas, thoughtfully stroking chin, his eyes peering suspiciously from one to the other.)*

**LOMBARD.** Where the devil did that voice come from?

*(They stare all round. **LOMBARD** goes into study up right.)*

Here we are.

**VOICE.** You are charged with these indictments –

**VERA.** Turn it off! Turn it off! It's horrible!

*(**LOMBARD** switches it off. **MRS. ROGERS** groans.)*

**ARMSTRONG.** A disgraceful and heartless practical joke.

**WARGRAVE.** *(with significance)* So you think it's a joke, do you?

**ARMSTRONG.** What else could it be?

*(**EMILY** sits down right.)*

**WARGRAVE.** *(with significance)* At the moment I'm not prepared to give an opinion.

*(**ROGERS** enters left 2 with brandy and glass on tray, puts it on table up left.)*

**MARSTON.** Who the devil turned it on, though? And set it going?

**WARGRAVE.** We must enquire into that. *(He looks significantly at **ROGERS**.)*

*(**LOMBARD** enters up right with record; puts it on chair right center. **MRS. ROGERS** begins to move and twist.)*

**MRS. ROGERS.** Oh, dear me! Oh, dear me!

*(The others move nearer, obscuring table where the brandy is. Attention is focused on **MRS. ROGERS**.)*

**ROGERS.** *(above sofa)* Allow me, Madam. *(to **ARMSTRONG**)* Allow me, sir. If I speak to her – Ethel – Ethel – *(His tone is urgent and nervous.)* It's all right. All right, do you hear? Pull yourself together.

(MRS. ROGERS *begins to gasp and moan. She tries to pull herself up; her frightened eyes stare round the room.*)

ARMSTRONG. *(taking wrist)* You'll be all right now, Mrs. Rogers. Just a nasty turn.

(BLORE *pours out brandy up left.*)

MRS. ROGERS. Did I faint, sir?

ARMSTRONG. Yes.

MRS. ROGERS. It was the voice – the awful voice – like a judgment –

(ROGERS *makes anxious movement.* MRS. ROGERS' *eyelids flutter. She seems about to collapse again.*)

ARMSTRONG. Where's the brandy?

(*They draw back a little, disclosing it.* BLORE *gives a glass to* VERA, *who gives it to* ARMSTRONG. VERA *sits left edge of sofa, holding cushion under* MRS. ROGERS' *head.*)

Drink this, Mrs. Rogers.

MRS. ROGERS. *(She gulps a little, revives. She sits up again.)* I'm all right now. I just – gave me a turn.

ROGERS. *(quickly)* Of course it did. Gave me a turn too. Wicked lies it was. I'd like to know –

(WARGRAVE *at center deliberately clears his throat. It stops* ROGERS, *who stares at him nervously.* WARGRAVE *clears his throat again, looking hard at* ROGERS.)

WARGRAVE. Who was it put that record on the gramophone? Was it you, Rogers?

ROGERS. I was just obeying orders, sir, that's all.

WARGRAVE. Whose orders?

ROGERS. Mr. Owen's.

WARGRAVE. Let me get this quite clear. Mr. Owen's orders were – what exactly?

ROGERS. I was to put a record on the gramophone in the study. I'd find the records in the drawer in there. I was to start with that one, sir. I thought it was just to give you all some music.

**WARGRAVE.** *(skeptically)* A very remarkable story.

**ROGERS.** *(hysterically)* It's the truth, sir. Before Heaven, it's the truth. I didn't know what it was – not for a moment. It had a name on it. I thought it was just a piece of music.

(**WARGRAVE** *looks toward* **LOMBARD**, *who examines record.*)

**WARGRAVE.** Is there a title?

**LOMBARD.** *(grinning)* A title? Yes, sir. It's entitled "Swan Song."

*(It amuses him, but some of the others react nervously.)*

**MACKENZIE.** The whole thing is preposterous – preposterous! Slinging accusations about like this. Something must be done about it. This fellow Owen, whoever he is – *(moves up left)*

**EMILY.** That's just it. Who is he?

**WARGRAVE.** *(with authority)* That is exactly what we must go into very carefully. I should suggest that you get your wife to bed, Rogers. Then come back here.

**ROGERS.** Yes, sir.

**ARMSTRONG.** I'll give you a hand.

**VERA.** *(rising)* Will she be all right, Doctor?

**ARMSTRONG.** Yes, quite all right.

(**ARMSTRONG** *and* **ROGERS** *help* **MRS. ROGERS** *up and take her out left 1.*)

**MARSTON.** *(to* **WARGRAVE***)* Don't know about you, sir, but I feel I need another drink.

**WARGRAVE.** I agree.

**MARSTON.** I'll get them. *(goes down right)*

**MACKENZIE.** *(muttering angrily)* Preposterous – that's what it is – preposterous. *(sits up left)*

**MARSTON**. Whiskey for you, Sir Lawrence?

**EMILY**. *(sits right sofa)* I should like a glass of water, please.

**VERA**. Yes, I'll get it. I'll have a little whiskey too. *(crosses down right)*

*(VERA takes glass of water to* **EMILY**, *then sits right center with her own drink. They sip drinks without speaking, but they eye each other.* **ARMSTRONG** *enters left 1.)*

**ARMSTRONG**. She'll be all right. I've given her a sedative.

**BLORE**. *(crosses down left)* Now, then, Doctor, you'll want a drink after all this.

**ARMSTRONG**. No, thank you. I never touch it. *(sits down left)*

**BLORE**. Oh, so you said. You have this one, General? *(up left to* **MACKENZIE** *)*

*(**MARSTON** and **LOMBARD** refill their glasses.* **ROGERS** *enters left 1.* **WARGRAVE** *takes charge.* **ROGERS** *stands near door left 1; he is nervous. Everyone focuses attention on him.)*

**WARGRAVE**. *(center above sofas)* Now, then, Rogers, we must get to the bottom of this. Tell us what you know about Mr. Owen.

**ROGERS**. He owns this place, sir.

**WARGRAVE**. I am aware of that fact. What I want you to tell me is what you yourself know about the man.

**ROGERS**. I can't say, sir. You see, I've never seen him.

*(faint stir of interest)*

**MACKENZIE**. What d'you mean, you've never seen him?

**ROGERS**. We've only been here just under a week, sir, my wife and I. We were engaged by letter through a registry office. The Regina, in Plymouth.

**BLORE**. That's a high-class firm. We can check on that.

**WARGRAVE**. Have you got the letter?

**ROGERS**. The letter engaging us? Yes, sir.

*(hunts for it and hands it to* **WARGRAVE**, *who runs through it)*

**WARGRAVE.** Go on with your story.

**ROGERS.** We arrived here like the letter said, on the 4th. Everything was in order, plenty of food in stock and everything very nice. Just needed dusting and that.

**WARGRAVE.** What next?

**ROGERS.** Nothing, sir. That is. We got orders to prepare the rooms for a house party – eight. Then yesterday, by the morning post, I received another letter saying Mr. and Mrs. Owen might be detained and, if so, we was to do the best we could, and it gave the instructions about dinner and putting on the gramophone record. Here it is, sir. *(crosses center, ands over letter, retires up center)*

**WARGRAVE.** Hmm. Headed Ritz Hotel and typewritten.

*(**BLORE** steps up to him and takes letter out of his hands. **MARSTON** to left of **BLORE**. **MACKENZIE** rises; looks over **WARGRAVE**'s shoulder.)*

**BLORE.** Coronation machine Number Five. Quite new. No defects. Ensign paper – most common make. We shan't get much out of this. We might try it for fingerprints, but it's been handled too much.

**LOMBARD.** Quite the little detective.

*(**WARGRAVE** turns and looks at him sharply. **BLORE**'s manner has completely changed, so has his voice. **MACKENZIE** sits up left again. **LOMBARD** sits left sofa.)*

**MARSTON.** *(taking letter, moving down right)* Got some fancy Christian names, hasn't he? Ulick Norman Owen. Quite a mouthful.

**WARGRAVE.** *(takes letter from **MARSTON**; crosses left below sofa)* I am obliged to you, Mr. Marston. You have drawn my attention to a curious and suggestive point. *(He looks around in his court manner.)* I think the time has come for all of us to pool our information. It would be well for everybody to come forward with all the information they have regarding our unknown host. We are all his guests. I think it would be profitable if each one of us were to explain exactly how that came about.

*(There is a pause.)*

**EMILY.** *(rising)* There's something very peculiar about all this. I received a letter with a signature that was not very easy to read. It purported to be from a woman whom I had met at a certain summer resort two or three years ago. I took the name to be Ogden. I am quite certain that I have never met or become friendly with anyone of the name of Owen.

**WARGRAVE.** Have you got that letter, Miss Brent?

**EMILY.** Yes. I will fetch it for you. *(goes out left 1)*

**WARGRAVE.** *(to left of* VERA*)* Miss Claythorne?

**VERA.** *(rises)* I never actually met Mrs. Owen. I wanted a holiday post and I applied to a secretarial agency. Miss Grenfell's in London. I was offered this post and accepted.

**WARGRAVE.** And you were never interviewed by your prospective employer?

**VERA.** No. This is the letter. *(hands it to him, sits again chair right center)*

**WARGRAVE.** *(reading)* "Soldier Island, Sticklehaven, Devon. I have received your name from Miss Grenfell's Agency. I understand she knows you personally. I shall be glad to pay you the salary you ask, and shall expect you to take up your duties on August 8th. The train is the 12:10 from Paddington and you will be met at Oakbridge Station. I enclose five pounds for expenses. Yours truly, Una Nancy Owen"

*(*MARSTON *starts to go up right.)*

Mr. Marston?

**MARSTON.** Don't actually know the Owens. Got a wire from a pal of mine, Badger Berkely. Told me to roll up here. Surprised me a bit because I had an idea the old horse had gone to Norway. I haven't got the wire. *(to right window)*

**WARGRAVE.** Thank you. Doctor Armstrong?

**ARMSTRONG.** *(after a pause, rising and coming left center)*

In the circumstances, I think I may admit that my visit here was professional. Mr. Owen wrote me that he was worried about his wife's health – her nerves, to be precise. He wanted a report without her being alarmed. He therefore suggested that my visit should be regarded as that of an ordinary guest.

**WARGRAVE.** You had no previous acquaintance with the family?

**ARMSTRONG.** No.

**WARGRAVE.** But you had no hesitation in obeying the summons?

**ARMSTRONG.** A colleague of mine was mentioned and a very handsome fee was suggested. I was due for a holiday, anyway. *(rises; crosses to right to mantelpiece for cigarette)*

*(**EMILY** re-enters and hands letter to **WARGRAVE**, who unfolds it and reads. **EMILY** sits down left.)*

**WARGRAVE.** "Dear Miss Brent: I do hope you remember me. We were together at Bell Haven Guest House in August some years ago and we seemed to have so much in common. I am starting a guest house of my own on an island off the coast of Devon. I think there is really an opening for a place where there is good plain English cooking, and a nice old-fashioned type of person. None of this nudity and gramophones half the night. I shall be very glad if you could see your way to spending your summer holiday on Soldier Island – as my guest, of course. I suggest August 8th, 12:40 from Paddington to Oakbridge. Yours sincerely, U.N." Hmm. Yes, the signature is slightly ambiguous.

**LOMBARD.** *(rises, crosses to **VERA**, aside to her)* I like the nudity touch!

**WARGRAVE.** *(to above sofas, takes letter from pocket)* Here is my own decoy letter. From an old friend of mine, Lady Constance Culmington. She writes in her usual vague, incoherent way, urges me to join her here and refers to her host and hostess in the vaguest of terms.

*(ARMSTRONG right of WARGRAVE, MARSTON to right of ARMSTRONG to look at letter, MACKENZIE to left of WARGRAVE.)*

**LOMBARD.** *(with sudden excitement, staring at BLORE)* Look here, I've just thought of something

**WARGRAVE.** In a minute.

**LOMBARD.** But I –

**WARGRAVE.** We will take one thing at a time, if you don't mind, Captain Lombard. General MacKenzie?

*(BLORE sits right end of left sofa.)*

**MACKENZIE.** *(rather incoherently, pulling at mustache)* Got a letter – from this fellow Owen – thought I must have met him sometime at the Club – mentioned some old cronies of mine who were to be here – hoped I'd excuse informal invitation. Haven't kept the letter, I'm afraid. *(sits up left)*

**WARGRAVE.** And you, Captain Lombard?

**LOMBARD.** Same sort of thing. Invitation mentioning mutual friends. I haven't kept the letter either.

*(Pause. WARGRAVE turns his attention to BLORE; he looks at him for some minutes. When he speaks, his voice is silky and dangerous.)*

**WARGRAVE.** Just now we had a somewhat disturbing experience. An apparently disembodied voice spoke to us all by name, uttering certain definite accusations against us. We will deal with those accusations presently. At the moment I am interested in a minor point. Amongst the names received was that of William Henry Blore. But as far as we know, there is no one named Blore amongst us. The name of Davis was not mentioned. What have you to say about that, Mr. Davis?

**BLORE.** *(rises)* Cat's out of the bag, it seems. I suppose I'd better admit my name isn't Davis.

**WARGRAVE.** You are William Henry Blore?

**BLORE.** That's right.

**LOMBARD.** *(to right of* **BLORE***)* I will add something to that. Not only are you here under a false name, Mr. Blore, but in addition I've noticed this evening that you're a first-class liar. You claim to have come from Natal, South Africa. I know South Africa and Natal well, and I'm prepared to swear that you've never set foot there in your life.

*(All turn toward* **BLORE***.* **ARMSTRONG** *goes up right to window.)*

**BLORE.** You gentlemen have got me wrong. I'm an ex – C.I.D. man.

**LOMBARD.** Oh, a copper!

**BLORE.** I've got my credentials and I can prove it. I run a detective agency in Plymouth. I was put onto this job.

**WARGRAVE.** By whom?

**BLORE.** Why, Mr. Owen. Sent a very nice money order for expenses, and said I was to join the house party, posing as a guest. He also sent a list of all your names and said I was to keep an eye on you all.

**WARGRAVE.** Any reason given?

**BLORE.** Said Mrs. Owen had got some valuable jewels. *(pause)* Mrs. Owen, my foot! I don't believe there's any such person. *(goes down right to cabinet)*

**WARGRAVE.** *(sits left sofa)* Your conclusions are, I think, justified. *(looks down at letters)* Ulick Norman Owen, Una Nancy Owen. Each time, that is to say, U.N. Owen. Or, by a slight stretch of fancy, Unknown.

**VERA.** But it's fantastic! Mad!

**WARGRAVE.** *(rises, quietly)* Oh, yes, I've no doubt in my own mind that we have been invited here by a madman – probably a dangerous homicidal lunatic.

*(There is an appalled silence.)*

**ROGERS.** Oh, my gawd!

**WARGRAVE.** *(to back of left sofa)* Whoever it is who has enticed us here, that person has taken the trouble to find out a great deal about us. *(pause)* A very great deal. And out of his knowledge concerning us, he has made certain definite accusations.

*(Everybody more or less speaks at once.)*

BLORE. It's all very well to make accusations.

MACKENZIE. A pack of damn lies! Slander!

VERA. It's iniquitous! Wicked!

ROGERS. A lie – a wicked lie – we never did, neither of us –

MARSTON. Don't know what the damned fool was getting at –

*(Everybody stops speaking at once.)*

WARGRAVE. *(raises a hand for silence, sits left sofa)* I wish to say this. Our unknown friend accuses me of the murder of one Edward Seton. I remember Seton perfectly well. He came up before me for trial in June, 1930. He was charged with the murder of an elderly woman. He was very ably defended and made a good impression on the jury in the witness box. Nevertheless, on the evidence he was certainly guilty. I summed up accordingly and the jury brought in a verdict of guilty. In passing sentence of death, I fully concurred with this verdict. The appeal was lodged on the grounds of misdirection. The appeal was dismissed and the man was duly executed. *(pause)* I wish to say before you all that my conscience is perfectly clear on the matter. I did my duty and nothing more. I passed sentence on a rightly convicted murderer.

ARMSTRONG. *(a pause, then to above* WARGRAVE*)* Did you know Seton at all? I mean, personally.

WARGRAVE. *(looks at him; he hesitates a moment)* I knew nothing of Seton previous to the trial.

LOMBARD. *(low to* VERA*)* The old boy's lying. I'll swear he's lying.

*(*ARMSTRONG *to down right.)*

MACKENZIE. *(rises)* Fellow's a madman. Absolute madman. Got a bee in his bonnet. Got hold of the wrong end of the stick all round. *(to* **WARGRAVE***)* Best really to leave this sort of thing unanswered. However, feel I ought to say – no truth – no truth whatever in what he said about – er – young Arthur Richmond. Richmond was one of my officers. I sent him on reconnaissance in 1917. He was killed. Also like to say – resent very much – slur on my wife. Been dead a long time. Best woman in the world. Absolutely – Caesar's wife. *(He sits down again.)*

**MARSTON.** *(right center)* I've just been thinking – John and Lucy Combes. Must have been a couple of kids I ran over near Cambridge. Beastly bad luck.

**WARGRAVE.** *(acidly)* For them or for you?

**MARSTON.** Well, I was thinking – for me – but, of course, you're right, sir. It was damned bad luck for them too. Of course, it was pure accident. They rushed out of some cottage or other. I had my license suspended for a year. Beastly nuisance.

**ARMSTRONG.** This speeding's all wrong – all wrong. Young men like you are a danger to the community.

**MARSTON.** *(wanders to right window; picks up his glass, which is half-full)* Well, I couldn't help it. Just an accident.

**ROGERS.** Might I say a word, sir?

**LOMBARD.** Go ahead, Rogers.

**ROGERS.** There was a mention, sir, of me and Mrs. Rogers, and of Miss Jennifer Brady. There isn't a word of truth in it. We were with Miss Brady when she died. She was always in poor health, sir, always from the time we came to her. There was a storm, sir, the night she died. The telephone was out of order. We couldn't get the doctor to her. I went for him, sir, on foot. But he got there too late. We'd done everything possible for her, sir. Devoted to her, we were. Anyone will tell you the same. There was never a word said against us. Never a word.

**BLORE.** *(in a bullying manner)* Came into a nice little

something at her death, I suppose. Didn't you?

**ROGERS**. *(crosses down right to* **BLORE**, *stiffly)* Miss Brady left us a legacy in recognition of our faithful service. And why not, I'd like to know?

**LOMBARD**. *(right center, with meaning)* What about yourself, Mr. Blore?

**BLORE**. What about me?

**LOMBARD**. Your name was on the list.

**BLORE**. I know, I know. Lendor, you mean? That was the London & Commercial Bank robbery.

**WARGRAVE**. *(crosses right below sofa to mantelpiece, lights pipe)* I remember the name, though it didn't come before me. Lendor was convicted on your evidence. You were the police officer in charge of the case.

**BLORE**. *(up to him)* I was, my Lud.

**WARGRAVE**. Lendor got penal servitude for life and died in Dartmoor a year later. He was a delicate man.

**BLORE**. He was a crook. It was him put the night watchman out. The case was clear from the start.

**WARGRAVE**. *(slowly)* You were complimented, I think, on your able handling of the case.

**BLORE**. I got my promotion. *(pause)* I was only doing my duty.

**LOMBARD**. *(sits right on sofa)* Convenient word – duty.

*(There is a general suspicious movement.* **VERA** *rises, moves as if to cross left, sees* **EMILY**, *turns. She sits again chair right center.* **WARGRAVE** *moves up to window seat,* **ARMSTRONG** *to center window.)*

What about you, Doctor?

**ARMSTRONG**. *(shakes his head good-humoredly)* I'm at a loss to understand the matter. The name meant nothing to me – what was it? Close? Close? I really don't remember having a patient of that name – or its being connected with a death in any way. The thing's a complete mystery to me. Of course, it's a long time ago. *(pause)* It might possibly be one of my operation cases in hospital. They come too late, so many of these people. Then, when the patient dies, it's always the surgeon's fault.

**LOMBARD.** And then it's better to take up nerve cases and give up surgery. Some, of course, give up drink.

**ARMSTRONG.** I protest. You've no right to insinuate such things. I never touch alcohol.

**LOMBARD.** My dear fellow, I never suggested you did. Anyway, Mr. Unknown is the only one who knows all the facts.

(**WARGRAVE** *to left of* **VERA, BLORE** *to right of her*)

**WARGRAVE.** Miss Claythorne?

**VERA.** *(Starts. She has been sitting, staring in front of her. She speaks unemotionally and without feeling of any kind.)* I was nursery governess to Peter Hamilton. We were in Cornwall for the summer. He was forbidden to swim out far. One day, when my attention was distracted, he started off – as soon as I saw what happened I swam after him. I couldn't get there in time –

**WARGRAVE.** Was there an inquest?

**VERA.** *(in the same dull voice)* Yes, I was exonerated by the Coroner. His mother didn't blame me either.

**WARGRAVE.** Thank you. *(crosses left)* Miss Brent?

**EMILY.** I have nothing to say.

**WARGRAVE.** Nothing?

**EMILY.** Nothing.

**WARGRAVE.** You reserve your defense?

**EMILY.** *(sharply)* There is no question of defense. I have always acted according to the dictates of my conscience. *(rises; moves up left)*

(**BLORE** *to fireplace*)

**LOMBARD.** What a law-abiding lot we seem to be! Myself excepted –

**WARGRAVE.** We are waiting for your story, Captain Lombard.

**LOMBARD.** I haven't got a story.

**WARGRAVE.** *(sharply)* What do you mean?

**LOMBARD.** *(grinning and apparently enjoying himself)* I'm sorry to disappoint all of you. It's just that I plead guilty. It's perfectly true. I left those natives alone in the bush. Matter of self-preservation.

*(His words cause a sensation.* **VERA** *looks at him unbelievingly.)*

**MACKENZIE.** *(rises, sternly)* You abandoned your men?

*(***EMILY*** *moves to window – seat up right)*

**LOMBARD.** *(coolly)* Not quite the act of a proper gentleman, I'm afraid. But after all, self-preservation's a man's first duty. And natives don't mind dying, you know. They don't feel about it as Europeans do – *(to right, sits fireplace fender)*

*(There is a pause.* **LOMBARD** *looks around at everyone with amusement.* **WARGRAVE** *clears throat disapprovingly.)*

**WARGRAVE.** Our inquiry rests there.

*(***ROGERS*** *crosses to left 1 door.)*

Now, Rogers, who else is there on this island besides ourselves and you and your wife?

**ROGERS.** Nobody, sir. Nobody at all.

**WARGRAVE.** You're sure of that?

**ROGERS.** Quite sure, sir.

**WARGRAVE.** Thank you.

*(***ROGERS*** *moves as if to go.)*

Don't go, Rogers. *(to everybody)* I am not yet clear as to the purpose of our unknown host in getting us to assemble here. But in my opinion he's not sane in the accepted sense of the word. He may be dangerous. In my opinion, it would be well for us to leave this place as soon as possible. I suggest that we leave here tonight.

*(General agreement,* **MACKENZIE** *sits up left.)*

**ROGERS**. I beg your pardon, sir, but there's no boat on the island.

**WARGRAVE**. No boat at all?

**ROGERS**. No, sir.

**WARGRAVE**. Why don't you telephone to the mainland?

**ROGERS**. There's no telephone. Fred Narracott, he comes over every morning, sir. He brings the milk and the bread and the post and the papers, and takes the orders.

**MARSTON**. *(picks up drink from window seat; crosses down right to front of right sofa, raising his voice)* A bit unsporting, what? Ought to ferret out the mystery before we go. Whole thing's like a detective story. Positively thrilling.

**WARGRAVE**. *(acidly)* At my time of life, I have no desire for thrills. *(sits down left)*

**(BLORE** *to left end sofa,* **MARSTON** *grins; stretches out his legs)*

**MARSTON**. The legal life's narrowing. I'm all for crime. *(raises his glass)* Here's to it.

*(Drinks it off at a gulp. Appears to choke – gasps – has a violent convulsion and slips onto sofa, glass falls from his hand.)*

**ARMSTRONG**. *(runs over to him, bends down, feels pulse, raises eyelid)* My God, he's dead!

**(MACKENZIE** *to left end sofa, the others can hardly take it in;* **ARMSTRONG** *sniffs lips, then sniffs glass, nods.)*

**MACKENZIE**. Dead? D'you mean the fellow just choked and died?

**ARMSTRONG**. You can call it choking if you like. He died of asphyxiation, right enough.

**MACKENZIE**. Never knew a man could die like that – just of a choking fit.

**EMILY**. *(with meaning)* In the middle of life we are in death.

*(She sounds inspired.)*

**ARMSTRONG.** A man doesn't die of a mere choking fit, General MacKenzie. Marston's death isn't what we call a natural death.

**VERA.** Was there something in the whiskey?

**ARMSTRONG.** Yes. By the smell of it, cyanide. Probably potassium cyanide. Acts pretty well instantaneously.

**LOMBARD.** Then he must have put the stuff in the glass himself.

**BLORE.** Suicide, eh? That's a rum go.

**VERA.** You'd never think he'd commit suicide. He was so alive. He was enjoying himself.

*(**EMILY** comes down and picks up remains of soldier from behind chair right center)*

**EMILY.** Oh! Look – here's one of the little soldiers off the mantelpiece – broken. *(holds it up)*

*(curtain)*

in book it is in
the dining room

# ACT TWO

## Scene I

*(The same, the following morning. The windows are open and the room has been tidied. It is a fine morning. There are only eight soldiers on the mantelpiece. Suitcases are piled up on the balcony. All are waiting for the boat to arrive.* MACKENZIE *is sitting up left in his chair, looking definitely a little queer.* EMILY *is sitting right center, knitting, with her hat and coat on.* WARGRAVE *is sitting window seat up right, a little apart, and is thoughtful. His manner is judicial throughout scene.* VERA, *by window center, is restless. She comes into the room as if to speak, no one takes any notice, goes down left and sits.* ARMSTRONG *and* BLORE *come up right on balcony.)*

ARMSTRONG. We've been up to the top. No sign of that boat yet.

VERA. It's very early still.

BLORE. Oh, I know. Still the fellow brings the milk and the bread and all that. I should have thought he'd have got here before this. *(opens door right 2 and looks in)* No sign of breakfast yet. Where's that fellow Rogers?

VERA. Oh, don't let's bother about breakfast

WARGRAVE. How's the weather looking?

BLORE. *(to window center)* The wind has freshened a bit. Rather a mackerel sky. Old boy in the train yesterday said we were due for dirty weather. Shouldn't wonder if he wasn't right –

ARMSTRONG. *(up center, nervously)* I wish that boat would come. The sooner we get off this island the better. It's absurd not keeping a boat on the island.

**BLORE.** No proper harbor. If the wind comes to blow from the southeast, a boat would get dashed to pieces against the rocks.

**EMILY.** But a boat would always be able to make us from the mainland?

**BLORE.** *(to left of* EMILY*)* No, Miss Brent – that's just what it wouldn't.

**EMILY.** Do you mean we should be cut off from the land?

**BLORE.** Yes. Condensed milk, ryvita and tinned stuff till the gale had blown itself out. But you needn't worry. The sea's only a bit choppy.

**EMILY.** I think the pleasures of living on an island are rather overrated.

**ARMSTRONG.** *(restless)* I wonder if that boat's coming. Annoying the way the house is built slap up against the cliff. You can't see the mainland until you've climbed to the top. *(to* **BLORE***)* Shall we go up there again?

**BLORE.** *(grinning)* It's no good. Doctor. A watched pot never boils. There wasn't a sign of a boat putting out when we were up there just now.

**ARMSTRONG.** *(to down right)* What can this man Narracott be doing?

**BLORE.** *(philosophically)* They're all like that in Devon. Never hurry themselves.

**ARMSTRONG.** And where's Rogers? He ought to be about.

**BLORE.** If you ask me, Master Rogers was pretty badly rattled last night.

**ARMSTRONG.** I know. *(shivers)* Ghastly – the whole thing.

**BLORE.** Got the wind up properly. I'd take an even bet that he and his wife did do that old lady in.

**WARGRAVE.** *(incredulous)* You really think so?

**BLORE.** Well, I never saw a man more scared. Guilty as hell, I should say.

**ARMSTRONG.** Fantastic – the whole thing – fantastic.

**BLORE**. I say, suppose he's hopped it?

**ARMSTRONG**. Who, Rogers? But there isn't any way he could. There's no boat on the island. You've just said so.

**BLORE**. Yes, but I've been thinking. We've only Rogers' word for that. Suppose there is one and he's nipped off in it the first thing.

**MACKENZIE**. Oh! No. He wouldn't be allowed to leave the island.

*(His tone is so strange they stare at him.)*

**BLORE**. Sleep well, General? *(crosses right of* **MACKENZIE***)*

**MACKENZIE**. I dreamed – yes, I dreamed –

**BLORE**. I don't wonder at that.

**MACKENZIE**. I dreamed of Lesley – my wife, you know.

**BLORE**. *(embarrassed)* Oh – er – yes – I wish Narracott would come. *(turns up to window)*

**MACKENZIE**. Who is Narracott?

**BLORE**. The bloke who brought us over yesterday afternoon.

**MACKENZIE**. Was it only yesterday?

**BLORE**. *(comes down center, determinedly cheerful)* Yes, I feel like that, too. Batty gramophone records – suicides – it's about all a man can stand. I shan't be sorry to see the back of Soldier Island, I give you my word.

**MACKENZIE**. So you don't understand. How strange!

**BLORE**. What's that, General?

*(**MACKENZIE** nods his head gently. **BLORE** looks questioningly at **ARMSTRONG**, then taps his forehead significantly.)*

**ARMSTRONG**. I don't like the look of him.

**BLORE**. I reckon young Marston's suicide must have been a pretty bad shock to him. He looks years older.

**ARMSTRONG**. Where is that poor young fellow now?

**BLORE**. In the study – put him there myself.

**VERA.** Doctor Armstrong, I suppose it was suicide?

**ARMSTRONG.** *(sharply)* What else could it be?

**VERA.** *(rises; crosses to right sofa; sits)* I don't know. But suicide – *(She shakes her head.)*

**BLORE.** *(crosses to behind left sofa)* You know, I had a pretty funny feeling in the night. This Mr. Unknown Owen, suppose he's on the island. Rogers mayn't know. *(pause)* Or he may have told him to say so. *(watches* **ARMSTRONG***)* Pretty nasty thought, isn't it?

**ARMSTRONG.** But would it have been possible for anyone to tamper with Marston's drink without our seeing him?

**BLORE.** Well, it was standing up there. Anyone could have slipped a dollop of cyanide in it if they'd wanted to.

**ARMSTRONG.** But that –

**ROGERS.** *(comes running up from right on balcony, he is out of breath, comes straight to* **ARMSTRONG***)* Oh, there you are, sir. I've been all over the place looking for you. Could you come up and have a look at my wife, sir?

**ARMSTRONG.** Yes, of course. *(goes toward door left 1)* Is she feeling under the weather still?

**ROGERS.** She's – she's – *(swallows convulsively; exits left 1)*

**ARMSTRONG.** You won't leave the island without me? *(***ARMSTRONG*** exits left 1.)*

**VERA.** *(rises, to left of windows)* I wish the boat would come. I hate this place.

**WARGRAVE.** Yes. I think the sooner we can get in touch with the police the better.

**VERA.** The police?

**WARGRAVE.** The police have to be notified in a case of suicide, you know, Miss Claythorne.

**VERA.** Oh, yes – of course. *(looks up right toward the door of study and shivers)*

**BLORE.** *(opening door left 2)* What's going on here? No sign of any breakfast.

**VERA.** Are you hungry, General?

(**MACKENZIE** *does not answer; she speaks louder.*)

Feeling like breakfast?

**MACKENZIE.** *(turns sharply)* Lesley – Lesley – my dear.

**VERA.** No – I'm not – I'm Vera Claythorne.

**MACKENZIE.** *(passes a hand over his eyes)* Of course. Forgive me. I took you for my wife.

**VERA.** Oh!

**MACKENZIE.** I was waiting for her, you see.

**VERA.** But I thought your wife was dead – long ago.

**MACKENZIE.** Yes. I thought so, too. But I was wrong. She's here. On this island.

**LOMBARD.** *(comes in from hall left 1)* Good morning.

(**VERA** *to above left sofa*)

**BLORE.** *(coming to down left)* Good morning, Captain Lombard.

**LOMBARD.** Good morning. Seem to have overslept myself. Boat here yet?

**BLORE.** No.

**LOMBARD.** Bit late, isn't it?

**BLORE.** Yes.

**LOMBARD.** *(to* **VERA***)* Good morning. You and I could have had a swim before breakfast. Too bad all this.

**VERA.** Too bad you overslept yourself.

**BLORE.** You must have good nerves to sleep like that.

**LOMBARD.** Nothing makes me lose my sleep.

(**VERA** *to mantelpiece*)

**BLORE.** Didn't dream of African natives, by any chance, did you?

**LOMBARD.** No. Did you dream of convicts on Dartmoor?

**BLORE.** *(angrily)* Look here, I don't think that's funny, Captain Lombard.

**LOMBARD.** Well, you started it, you know. I'm hungry. What about breakfast? *(to left sofa – sits)*

**BLORE.** The whole domestic staff seems to have gone on strike.

**LOMBARD.** Oh, well, we can always forage for ourselves.

**VERA.** *(examining soldier figures)* Hullo, that's strange.

**LOMBARD.** What is?

**VERA.** You remember we found one of these little fellows smashed last night?

**LOMBARD.** Yes – that ought to leave nine.

**VERA.** That ought to leave nine. I'm certain there were ten of them here when we arrived.

**LOMBARD.** Well?

**VERA.** There are only eight.

**LOMBARD.** *(looking)* So there are. *(to mantelpiece)*

*(They look at each other.)*

**VERA.** I think its queer, don't you?

**LOMBARD.** Probably only were nine to begin with. We assumed there were ten because of the rhyme.

*(**ARMSTRONG** enters left 1. He is upset, but striving to appear calm; shuts door and stands against it.)*

Hullo, Armstrong, what's the matter?

**ARMSTRONG.** Mrs. Rogers is dead.

*(**WARGRAVE** rises)*

**BLORE & VERA.** No? How?

*(**VERA** to right end left sofa)*

**ARMSTRONG.** Died in her sleep. Rogers thought she was still under the influence of the sleeping draught I gave her and came down without disturbing her. He lit the kitchen fire and did this room. Then, as she hadn't appeared, he went up, was alarmed by the look of her and went hunting for me. *(pause)* She's been dead about five hours, I should say.

*(sits down left; **VERA** sits left sofa)*

**BLORE**. What was it? Heart?

**ARMSTRONG**. Impossible to say. It may have been.

**BLORE**. After all, she had a pretty bad shock last night.

**ARMSTRONG**. Yes.

**WARGRAVE**. *(comes down to left end of right sofa)* She might have been poisoned, I suppose, Doctor?

**ARMSTRONG**. It is perfectly possible.

**WARGRAVE**. With the same stuff as young Marston?

**ARMSTRONG**. No, not cyanide. It would have to have been some narcotic or hypnotic. One of the barbiturates, or chloral. Something like that.

**BLORE**. You gave her some sleeping powders last night, didn't you?

**ARMSTRONG**. *(rises, crossing to cabinet right for drink of water)* Yes, I gave her a mild dose of Luminal.

**BLORE**. Didn't give her too much, did you?

**ARMSTRONG**. Certainly not. What do you mean?

**BLORE**. All right – no offense, no offense. I just thought that perhaps if she'd had a weak heart –

**ARMSTRONG**. The amount I gave her could not have hurt anyone.

**LOMBARD**. Then what exactly did happen?

**ARMSTRONG**. Impossible to say without an autopsy.

**WARGRAVE**. If, for instance, this death had occurred in the case of one of your private patients, what would have been your procedure?

**ARMSTRONG**. *(crossing left, sits down left)* Without any previous knowledge of the woman's state of health, I could certainly not give a certificate.

**VERA**. She was a very nervous-looking creature. She had a bad fright last night. Perhaps it was heart failure.

**ARMSTRONG**. Her heart certainly failed to beat – but what caused it to fail?

**EMILY**. *(firmly and with emphasis)* Conscience.

*(They all jump and look at her.* **WARGRAVE** *to right.)*

**ARMSTRONG.** What exactly do you mean by that, Miss Brent?

**EMILY.** You all heard – she was accused, together with her husband, of having deliberately murdered her former employer – an old lady.

**BLORE.** And you believe that's true, Miss Brent?

**EMILY.** Certainly. You all saw her last night. She broke down completely and fainted. The shock of having her wickedness brought home to her was too much for her. She literally died of fear.

**ARMSTRONG.** *(doubtfully)* It is a possible theory. One cannot adopt it without more exact knowledge of her state of health. If there was a latent cardiac weakness –

**EMILY.** Call it, if you prefer, An Act of God.

*(Everyone is shocked.)*

**BLORE.** Oh, no, Miss Brent. *(moves up left)*

*(**LOMBARD** to window)*

**EMILY.** *(emphatically)* You regard it as impossible that a sinner should be struck down by the wrath of God? I do not.

**WARGRAVE.** *(strokes his chin, his voice is ironic, coming down right)* My dear lady, in my experience of ill doing, Providence leaves the work of conviction and chastisement to us mortals – and the process is often fraught with difficulties. There are no short cuts.

**BLORE.** Let's be practical. What did the woman have to eat and drink last night after she went to bed?

**ARMSTRONG.** Nothing.

**BLORE.** Nothing at all? Not a cup of tea? Or a glass of water? I'll bet you she had a cup of tea. That sort always does.

**ARMSTRONG.** Rogers assures me she had nothing whatever.

**BLORE.** He might say so.

**LOMBARD.** So that's your idea?

**BLORE.** Well, why not? You heard that accusation last night.

*[handwritten margin note: to reprimand]*

What if it's true? Miss Brent thinks it is, for one. Rogers and his missus did the old lady in. They're feeling quite safe and happy about it –

VERA. Happy?

BLORE. *(sits left sofa)* Well – they know there's no immediate danger to them. Then, last night some lunatic goes and spills the beans. What happens? It's the woman cracks. Goes to pieces. Did you see him hanging round her when she was coming to? Not all husbandly solicitude? Not on your sweet life. He was like a cat on hot bricks. And that's the position. They've done a murder and got away with it. But if it's all going to be raked up again now, it's the woman will give the show away. She hadn't got the nerve to brazen it out. She's a living danger to her husband, that's what she is, and him – he's all right. He'll go on lying till the cows come home, but he can't be sure of her. So what does he do? He drops a nice little dollop of something into a nice cup of tea, and when she's had it, he washes up the cup and saucer and tells the doctor she ain't had nothing.

VERA. Oh, no. That's impossible. A man wouldn't do that – not to his wife. *(rises; goes up left)*

BLORE. You'd be surprised, Miss Claythorne, what some husbands would do. *(rises)*

ROGERS. *(Enters left 2. He is dead-white and speaks like an automaton, just the mask of the trained servant, to VERA.)* Excuse me, Miss, I'm getting on with breakfast. I'm not much of a hand as a cook, I'm afraid. It's lunch that's worrying me. Would cold tongue and gelatin be satisfactory? And I could manage some fried potatoes. And then there's tinned fruit and cheese and biscuits.

VERA. That will be fine, Rogers.

BLORE. Lunch? Lunch? We shan't be here for lunch! And when the hell's that boat corning?

EMILY. Mr. Blore! *(picks up her case and marches up to right window seat; sits)*

**BLORE.** What?

**ROGERS.** *(fatalistically)* You'll pardon me, sir, but the boat won't be coming.

**BLORE.** What?

**ROGERS.** Fred Narracott's always here before eight. *(pause)* Is there anything else you require, Miss?

**VERA.** No, thank you, Rogers.

(**ROGERS** *goes out left 2*)

**BLORE.** And it's not Rogers! His wife lying dead upstairs and there he's cooking breakfast and calmly talking about lunch! Now he says the boat won't be corning. How the 'ell does he know?

**EMILY.** Mr. Blore!

**BLORE.** What?

**VERA.** *(crossing down left)* Oh, don't you see? He's dazed. He's just carrying on automatically as a good servant would. It's – it's pathetic, really.

**BLORE.** He's pulling a fast one, if you ask me.

**WARGRAVE.** The really significant thing is the failure of the boat to arrive. It means that we are being deliberately cut off from help.

**MACKENZIE.** That's very little time – very little time –

**BLORE.** What's that, General?

**MACKENZIE.** *(rising)* Very little time. We mustn't waste it talking about things that don't matter.

(*He turns to window. They all look at him dubiously before resuming.*)

**LOMBARD.** *(down right to* **WARGRAVE***)* Why do you think Narracott hasn't turned up?

**WARGRAVE.** I think the ubiquitous Mr. Owen has given orders.

**LOMBARD.** You mean, told him it's a practical joke or something of that kind?

**BLORE**. He'd never fall for that, would he?

**LOMBARD**. Why not? Soldier Island's got a reputation for people having crazy parties. This is just one more crazy idea, that's all. Narracott knows there's plenty of food and drink in the island. Probably thinks it's all a huge joke.

**VERA**. Couldn't we light a bonfire up on the top of the island? So that they'd see it?

**LOMBARD**. That's probably been provided against. All signals are to be ignored. We're cut off all right.

**VERA**. *(impatiently)* But can't we do something?

**LOMBARD**. Oh, yes, we can do something. We can find the funny gentleman who's staged this little joke, Mr. Unknown Owen. I'll bet anything you like he's somewhere on the island, and the sooner we get hold of him the better. Because, in my opinion, he's mad as a hatter. And as dangerous as a rattlesnake.

**WARGRAVE**. Hardly a very good simile, Captain Lombard. The rattlesnake at least gives warning of its approach.

**LOMBARD**. Warning? My God, yes! *(indicating nursery rhyme)* That's our warning. *(reading:)* "Ten little soldier boys – "

There were ten of us after Narracott went, weren't there?

"Ten little soldier boys going out to dine; One went and choked himself – "

Marston choked himself, didn't he? And then –

"Nine little soldier boys sat up very late. One overslept himself – "

Overslept himself – the last part fits Mrs. Rogers rather well, doesn't it?

**VERA**. You don't think – ? Do you mean that he wants to kill us all?

**LOMBARD**. Yes, I think he does.

**VERA**. And each one fits with the rhyme!

**ARMSTRONG**. No, no, it's impossible. It's coincidence. It must be coincidence.

**LOMBARD.** Only eight little soldier boys here. I suppose that's coincidence too. What do you think, Blore?

**BLORE.** I don't like it.

**ARMSTRONG.** But there's nobody on the island.

**BLORE.** I'm not so sure of that.

**ARMSTRONG.** This is terrible.

**MACKENZIE.** None of us will ever leave this island.

**BLORE.** Can't somebody shut up Grandpa?

**LOMBARD.** Don't you agree with me, Sir Lawrence?

**WARGRAVE.** *(slowly)* Up to a point – yes.

**LOMBARD.** Then the sooner we get to work the better. Come on, Armstrong. Come on, Blore. We'll make short work of it.

**BLORE.** I'm ready. Nobody's got a revolver, by any chance? I suppose that's too much to hope for.

**LOMBARD.** I've got one. *(takes it out of pocket)*

**BLORE.** *(BLORE's eyes open rather wide; an idea occurs to him – not a pleasant one.)* Always carry that about with you?

**LOMBARD.** Usually. I've been in some tight places, you know.

**BLORE.** Oh. Well, you've probably never been in a tighter place than you are today. If there's a homicidal maniac hiding on this island, he's probably got a whole arsenal on him – and he'll use it.

**ARMSTRONG.** You may be wrong there, Blore. Many homicidal maniacs are very quiet, unassuming people.

**WARGRAVE.** Delightful fellows!

**ARMSTRONG.** You'd never guess there was anything wrong with them.

**BLORE.** If Mr. Owen turns out to be one of that kind, we'll leave him to you, Doctor. Now, then, let's make a start. I suggest Captain Lombard searches the house while we do the island.

**LOMBARD.** right. House ought to be easy. No sliding panels or secret doors. *(goes up right toward study)*

**BLORE**. Mind he doesn't get you before you get him!

**LOMBARD**. Don't worry. But you two had better stick together – remember – "One got left behind."

**BLORE**. Come on, Armstrong.

*(They go along and out up right.)*

**WARGRAVE**. *(rises)* A very energetic young man, Captain Lombard.

**VERA**. *(to up left)* Don't you think he's right? If someone is hiding on the island, they'll be bound to find him. It's practically bare rock.

**WARGRAVE**. I think this problem needs brains to solve it. Rather than brawn. *(goes toward balcony)*

**VERA**. Where are you going?

**WARGRAVE**. I'm going to sit in the sun – and think, my dear young lady. *(goes up right on balcony)*

**EMILY**. Where did I put that skein of wool? *(gets up and comes down right)*

**VERA**. Did you leave it upstairs? Shall I go and see if I can find it?

**EMILY**. No, I'll go. I know where it's likely to be. *(Goes out left 1)*

**VERA**. I'm glad Captain Lombard has got a revolver.

**MACKENZIE**. They're all wasting time – wasting time.

**VERA**. Do you think so?

**MACKENZIE**. Yes, it's much better to sit quietly – and wait.

**VERA**. Wait for what? *(sits left sofa)*

**MACKENZIE**. For the end, of course. *(There is a pause, **MACKENZIE** rises, opens and shuts both doors left.)* I wish I could find Lesley.

**VERA**. Your wife?

**MACKENZIE**. *(crosses up right, below right sofa)* Yes. I wish you'd known her. She was so pretty. So gay –

**VERA**. Was she?

**MACKENZIE**. I loved her very much. Of course, I was a lot older than she was. She was only twenty-seven, you know. *(pause)* Arthur Richmond was twenty-six. He was my A.D.C. *(pause)* Lesley liked him. They used to talk of music and plays together, and she teased him and made fun of him. I was pleased. I thought she took a motherly interest in the boy. *(suddenly to* **VERA,** *confidentially)* Damn fool, wasn't I? No fool like an old fool. *(a long pause)* Exactly like a book the way I found out. When I was out in France. She wrote to both of us, and she put the letters in the wrong envelope. *(He nods his head.)* So I knew –

**VERA.** *(in pity)* Oh, no.

**MACKENZIE.** *(sits right sofa)* It's all right, my dear. It's a long time ago. But you see I loved her very much – and believed in her. I didn't say anything to him – I let it gather inside – here – *(strikes chest)* a slow, murderous rage – damned young hypocrite – I'd liked the boy – trusted him.

**VERA.** *(trying to break the spell)* I wonder what the others are doing?

**MACKENZIE.** I sent him to his death.

**VERA.** Oh –

**MACKENZIE.** It was quite easy. Mistakes were being made all the time. All anyone could say was that I'd lost my nerve a bit, made a blunder, sacrificed one of my best men. Yes, it was quite easy *(pause)* Lesley never knew. I never told her I'd found out. We went on as usual – but somehow nothing was quite real any more. She died of pneumonia. *(pause)* She had a heart-shaped face-and grey eyes – and brown hair that curled.

**VERA.** Oh, don't.

**MACKENZIE.** *(rises)* Yes, I suppose in a way – it was murder. Curious, murder – and I've always been such a law-abiding man. It didn't feel like that at the time. "Serves him damn well right!" that's what I thought. But after – *(pause)* Well, you know, don't you?

**VERA.** *(at a loss)* What do you mean?

**MACKENZIE.** *(stares at her as though something puzzles him)* You don't seem to understand – I thought you would. I thought you'd be glad, too, that the end was coming –

**VERA.** *(draws back, alarmed; rises, backs down left)* I – *(She eyes him warily.)*

**MACKENZIE.** *(follows her confidentially)* We're all going to die, you know.

**VERA.** *(looking round for help)* I – I don't know.

**MACKENZIE.** *(vaguely to* **VERA***)* You're very young – you haven't got to that yet. The relief! The blessed relief when you know that you've done with it all, that you haven't got to carry the burden any longer. *(moves up right)*

**VERA.** *(follows him – moved)* General –

**MACKENZIE.** Don't talk to me that way. You don't understand. I want to sit here and wait – wait for Lesley to come for me.

*(Goes out on balcony and draws up chair and sits, the back of his head down to shoulders is visible through window. His position does not change throughout the scene.)*

**VERA.** *(stares after him, her composure breaks down, sits left sofa)* I'm frightened – oh! I'm frightened –

*(***LOMBARD*** comes in up right)*

**LOMBARD.** *(crosses left)* All correct. No secret passage – one corpse.

**VERA.** *(tensely)* Don't!

**LOMBARD.** I say, you do look low. How about a drink to steady your nerves?

**VERA.** *(rises, flaring up)* A drink! Two corpses in the house at nine o'clock in the morning and all you say, "Have a drink!" An old man going quite crackers – "Have a drink!" Ten people accused of murder – that's all right – just have a drink. Everything's fine so long as you have a drink.

**LOMBARD.** All right. All right – stay thirsty. *(goes to left 2 door)*

**VERA.** Oh, you – you're nothing but a waster – an adventurer – you make me tired. *(moves to fireplace)*

**LOMBARD.** *(crossing to her)* I say, you are bet up. What's the matter, my sweet?

**VERA.** I'm not your sweet.

**LOMBARD.** I'm sorry. I rather thought you were.

**VERA.** Well, you can think again.

**LOMBARD.** Come now – you know you don't really feel like that. We've got something in common, you and I. Rogues and murderers can't fall out.

*(H.e takes her hand, she draws away)*

**VERA.** Rogues and murderers – !

**LOMBARD.** Okay. You don't like the company of rogues and murderers – and you won't have a drink. I'll go and finish searching – *(exits left 1)*

*(**EMILY** enters left 1, **VERA** moves up to window)*

**EMILY.** Unpleasant young man! I can't find it anywhere. *(sees **VERA**'s face)* Is anything the matter? *(to above left sofa)*

**VERA.** *(low)* I'm worried about the General. He really is ill, I think.

**EMILY.** *(looks from **VERA** to **MACKENZIE**, then goes out on balcony and stands behind him. in loud, cheerful voice, as though talking to an idiot child)* Looking out for the boat, General?

*(**VERA** to down left, **MACKENZIE** does not answer. **EMILY** waits a minute, then comes slowly in, unctuously)*

His sin has found him out.

**VERA.** *(angrily)* Oh, don't.

**EMILY.** One must face facts.

**VERA.** Can any of us afford to throw stones?

**EMILY.** *(comes down center; sits right sofa)* Even if his wife was no better than she should be – and she must have been a depraved woman – he had no right to take judgment into his own hands.

**VERA.** *(coldly angry)* What about – Beatrice Taylor?

**EMILY.** Who?

**VERA.** That was the name, wasn't it? *(looks at her challengingly)*

**EMILY.** You are referring to that absurd accusation about myself?

**VERA.** Yes.

**EMILY.** Now that we are alone, I have no objection to telling you the facts of the case – Indeed I should like you to hear them.

*(VERA sits left sofa)*

It was not a fit subject to discuss before gentlemen – so naturally I refused to say anything last night. That girl, Beatrice Taylor, was in my service. I was very much deceived in her. She had nice manners and was clean and willing. I was very pleased with her. Of course, all that was sheerest hypocrisy. She was a loose girl with no morals. Disgusting! It was some time before I found out that she was what they call "in trouble." *(pause)* It was a great shock to me. Her parents were decent folks too, who had brought her up strictly. I'm glad to say they didn't condone her behavior.

**VERA.** What happened?

**EMILY.** *(self-righteously)* Naturally, I refused to keep her an hour under my roof. No one shall ever say I condoned immorality.

**VERA.** Did she drown herself?

**EMILY.** Yes.

**VERA.** *(rises to left)* How old was she?

**EMILY.** Seventeen.

**VERA.** Only seventeen.

**EMILY.** *(with horrible fanaticism)* Quite old enough to know how to behave. I told her what a low depraved thing she was. I told her that she was beyond the pale and that no decent person would take her into their house. I told her that her child would be the child of sin and would be branded all its life – and that the man would naturally not dream of marrying her. I told her that I felt soiled by ever having her under my roof –

**VERA**. *(shuddering)* You told a girl of seventeen all that?

**EMILY**. Yes. I'm glad to say I broke her down utterly.

**VERA**. Poor little devil.

**EMILY**. I've no patience with this indulgence toward sin.

**VERA**. *(moves up left to above sofa)* And then, I suppose, you turned her out of the house?

**EMILY**. Of course.

**VERA**. And she didn't dare go home – *(comes down right to center)* What did you feel like when you found she'd drowned herself?

**EMILY**. *(puzzled)* Feel like?

**VERA**. Yes. Didn't you blame yourself?

**EMILY**. Certainly not. I had nothing with which to reproach myself.

**VERA**. I believe – I believe you really feel like that. That makes it even more horrible. *(turns away to right, then goes up to center windows)*

**EMILY**. That girl's unbalanced. *(opens bag and takes out a small Bible, begins to read it in a low mutter)* "The heathen are sunk down in the pit that they made – *(stops and nods her head)* In the net which they hid is their own foot taken."

(**ROGERS** *enters left 2.* **EMILY** *stops and smiles approvingly.*)

"The Lord is known by the judgment He executeth, the wicked is snared in the work of his own hand."

**ROGERS**. *(looks doubtfully at* **EMILY***)* Breakfast is ready.

**EMILY.** "The wicked shall be turned into hell." *(turns head sharply)* Be quiet.

**ROGERS.** Do you know where the gentlemen are, Miss? Breakfast is ready. *(to above left sofa)*

**VERA.** Sir Lawrence Wargrave is sitting out there in the sun. Doctor Armstrong and Mr. Blore are searching the island. I shouldn't bother about them. *(She comes in.)*

*(**ROGERS** goes out to balcony.)*

**EMILY.** "Shall not the isles shake at the sound of the fall, when the wounded cry, when the slaughter is made in the midst of thee?"

**VERA.** *(to left, coldly, after waiting a minute or two)* Shall we go in?

**EMILY.** I don't feel like eating.

**ROGERS.** *(to **MACKENZIE**)* Breakfast is ready. *(goes off right on balcony)*

**EMILY.** *(opens Bible again)* "Then all the princes of the sea shall come down from their thrones, and lay away their robes, and put off their 'broidered garments."

*(enter **BLORE**, up right)*

"They shall clothe themselves with trembling, they shall sit upon the ground, and shall tremble at every moment, and be astonished at thee."

*(looks up and sees **BLORE**, but her eyes are almost unseeing)*

**BLORE.** *(speaks readily, but watches her with a new interest)* Reading aloud, Miss Brent?

**EMILY.** It is my custom to read a portion of the Bible every day.

**BLORE.** Very good habit, I'm sure. *(to down right)*

*(**ARMSTRONG** comes right along balcony and in)*

**VERA.** What luck did you have?

ARMSTRONG. There's no cover in the island. No caves. No one could hide anywhere.

(*warn curtain*)

BLORE. That's right.

(**LOMBARD** *enters left 2*)

What about the house, Lombard?

LOMBARD. No one. I'll stake my life there's no one in the house but ourselves. I've been over it from attic to cellar.

(**ROGERS** *enters from balcony.* **WARGRAVE** *comes right along balcony, slowly, and in to right of window.*)

ROGERS. Breakfast is getting cold.

(**EMILY** *is still reading.*)

LOMBARD. (*boisterously*) Breakfast! Come on, Blore. You've been yelping for breakfast ever since you got up. Let's eat, drink and be merry, for tomorrow we die. Or who knows, perhaps, even today!

(**VERA** *and* **ARMSTRONG** *cross to left 2 door.*)

(**EMILY** *rises and drops the knitting.* **BLORE** *picks it up.*)

EMILY. You ought to be ashamed of such levity, Captain Lombard. (*crosses right*)

LOMBARD. (*still in the same vein, with determination*) Come on, General, can't have this. (*calls*) Breakfast, I say, sir –

(*Goes out on balcony to* **MACKENZIE**. *Stops – stoops – comes slowly back and stands in window. His face is stern and dangerous.*)

Good God! One got left behind – there's a knife in **MACKENZIE**'s back.

ARMSTRONG. (*goes to him*) He's dead – he's dead.

BLORE. But he can't be – Who could have done it? There's only us on the island.

Book = got hit in the head
            with a life saver

**WARGRAVE.** Exactly, my dear sir. Don't you realize that this clever and cunning criminal is always comfortably one stage ahead of us? That he knows exactly what we are going to do next, and makes his plans accordingly? There's only one place, you know, where a successful murderer could hide and have a reasonable chance of getting away with it.

**BLORE.** One place – where?

**WARGRAVE.** Here in this room – Mr. Owen is one of us!

*(curtain)*

### Scene II

*(There is a storm; the room is much darker – the windows closed and beating rain and wind. WARGRAVE comes in from left 2, followed by BLORE.)*

**BLORE.** Sir Lawrence?

**WARGRAVE.** *(center.)* Well, Mr. Blore?

**BLORE.** I wanted to get you alone. *(looks over shoulder at dining room)* You were right in what you said this morning. This damned murderer is one of us. And I think I know which one.

**WARGRAVE.** Really?

**BLORE.** Ever hear of the Lizzie Borden case? In America. Old couple killed with an axe in the middle of the morning. Only person who could have done it was the daughter, a respectable, middle-aged spinster. Incredible. So incredible that they acquitted her. But they never found any other explanation.

**WARGRAVE.** Then your answer to the problem is Miss Emily Brent?

**BLORE.** I tell you that woman is mad as a hatter. Religious mad, I tell you – she's the one. And we must watch her.

**WARGRAVE.** Really? I had formed the impression that your suspicions were in a different quarter.

**BLORE.** Yes – but I've changed my mind, and I'll tell you why – she's not scared and she's the only one who isn't. Why? Because she knows quite well she's in no danger – hush –

*(WARGRAVE goes up right. VERA and EMILY enter from left 2. VERA is carrying coffee tray, EMILY up center.)*

**VERA.** We've made some coffee.

*(She puts tray on tabouret right center. BLORE moves up to tabouret.)*

Brr – it's cold in here.

BLORE. You'd hardly believe it when you think what a beautiful day it was this morning.

VERA. Are Captain Lombard and Rogers still out?

BLORE. Yes. No boat will put out in this – and it couldn't land, anyway.

VERA. Miss Brent's. *(hands coffee cup to* **BLORE**)

*(EMILY comes down; sits left sofa)*

WARGRAVE. Allow me. *(takes cup and hands it to* **EMILY**)

VERA. *(to* **WARGRAVE**) You were right to insist on our going to lunch – and drinking some brandy with it. I feel better.

WARGRAVE. *(returns to coffee tray, takes his own coffee, stands by mantelpiece)* The court always adjourns for lunch.

VERA. All the same, it's a nightmare. It seems as though it can't be true. What – what are we going to do about it?

*(BLORE sits in chair right center.)*

WARGRAVE. We must hold an informal court of inquiry. We may at least be able to eliminate some innocent people.

BLORE. You haven't got a hunch of any kind, have you, Miss Claythorne?

WARGRAVE. If Miss Claythorne suspects one of us three, that is rather an awkward question.

VERA. I'm sure it isn't any of you. If you ask me who I suspected, I'd say Doctor Armstrong.

BLORE. Armstrong?

VERA Yes. Because, don't you see, he's had far and away the best chance to kill Mrs. Rogers. Terribly easy for him, as a doctor, to give her an overdose of sleeping stuff.

BLORE. That's true. But someone else gave her brandy, remember.

*(EMILY goes up left and sits.)*

WARGRAVE. Her husband had a good opportunity of administering a drug.

**BLORE**. It isn't Rogers. He wouldn't have the brains to fix all this stunt – nor the money. Besides you can see he's scared stiff.

(**ROGERS** *and* **LOMBARD**, *in mackintoshes, come up right on balcony and appear at window.* **BLORE** *goes and lets them in. As he opens the window, a swirl of loud wind and rain comes in.* **EMILY** *half screams and turns around.*)

**LOMBARD**. My God, it's something like a storm.

**EMILY**. Oh, it's only you –

**VERA**. Who did you think it was? *(pause)* Beatrice Taylor?

**EMILY**. *(angrily)* Eh?

**LOMBARD**. Not a hope of rescue until this dies down. Is that coffee? Good. *(to* **VERA***)* I'm taking to coffee now, you see.

**VERA**. *(takes him a cup)* Such restraint in the face of danger is nothing short of heroic.

**WARGRAVE**. *(crosses to down left; sits)* I do not, of course, profess to be a weather prophet. But I should say that it is very unlikely that a boat could reach us, even if it knew of our plight, under twenty – four hours. Even if the wind drops, the sea has still to go down.

(**LOMBARD** *sits left sofa.* **ROGERS** *pulls off his shoes.*)

**VERA**. You're awfully wet.

**BLORE**. Is anyone a swimmer? Would it be possible to swim to the mainland?

**VERA**. It's over a mile – and in this sea you'd be dashed on the rocks and drowned.

**EMILY**. *(speaking like one in a trance)* Drowned – drowned in the pond – *(drops knitting)*

**WARGRAVE**. *(rising; startled, moves up to her)* I beg your pardon, Miss Brent. *(He picks it up for her.)*

**BLORE**. After dinner nap.

(*another furious gust of wind and rain*)

**VERA**. It's terribly cold in here. *(to right; sits on fender)*

**ROGERS**. I could light the fire if you like, Miss?

**VERA**. That would be a good idea.

**LOMBARD**. *(crossing right)* Very sound scheme, Rogers. *(he sits on fender; puts on shoes)*

**ROGERS**. *(goes toward left door 1 – is going through but comes back and asks:)* Excuse me, but does anybody know what's become of the top bathroom curtain?

**LOMBARD**. Really, Rogers, are you going bats too?

**BLORE**. *(blankly)* The bathroom curtain?

**ROGERS**. Yes, sir. Scarlet oilsilk. It's missing.

*(They look at each other.)*

**LOMBARD**. Anybody seen a scarlet oilsilk curtain? No good, I'm afraid, Rogers.

**ROGERS**. It doesn't matter, sir, only I just thought as it was odd.

**LOMBARD**. Everything on this island is odd.

**ROGERS**. I'll get some sticks and a few knobs of coal and get a nice fire going. *(goes out left 2)*

**VERA**. I wonder if he would like some hot coffee. He's very wet. *(runs out after him, calling "Rogers")*

**LOMBARD**. What's become of Armstrong?

**WARGRAVE**. He went to his room to rest.

**LOMBARD**. Somebody's probably batted him one by now!

**WARGRAVE**. I expect he had the good sense to bolt his door.

**BLORE**. It won't be so easy now that we're all on our guard. *(lights cigarette at mantelpiece)*

*(a rather unpleasant silence)*

**WARGRAVE**. I advise you, Mr. Blore, not to be too confident. I should like shortly to propose certain measures of safety, which I think we should all adopt.

**LOMBARD**. Against whom?

**WARGRAVE**. *(up center)* Against each other. We are all in grave danger. Of the ten people who came to this island, three are definitely cleared. There are seven of us left – seven little soldier boys.

**LOMBARD.** One of whom is a bogus little soldier boy.

**WARGRAVE.** Exactly.

**BLORE.** *(to right center)* Well, in spite of what Miss Claythorne said just now, I'd say that you, Sir Lawrence, and Doctor Armstrong are above suspicion. He's a well – known doctor, and you're known all over England.

**WARGRAVE.** *(interrupts him)* Mr. Blore, that proves nothing at all. Judges have gone mad before now. So have doctors. *(pause)* So have policemen.

**LOMBARD.** Hear, hear. *(VERA enters left 2)* Well, does he want some coffee?

**VERA.** *(crossing right to tabouret right center, lightly)* He'd rather make himself a nice cup of tea! What about Doctor Armstrong? Do you think we ought to take him up a cup?

**WARGRAVE.** I will take it up if you like.

**LOMBARD.** I'll take it. I want to change.

**VERA.** Yes, you ought to. You'll catch cold.

**WARGRAVE.** *(smiling ironically)* I think Doctor Armstrong might prefer to see me. He might not admit you, Captain Lombard. He might be afraid of your revolver.

**BLORE.** Ah, the revolver. *(meaningly)* I want a word with you about that –

**VERA.** *(to LOMBARD)* Do go and change.

*(WARGRAVE takes a cup from her and, passing behind, goes out left 2.)*

**LOMBARD.** *(up right center to BLORE)* What were you going to say?

**BLORE.** I'd like to know why you brought a revolver down here on what's supposed to be a little social visit.

**LOMBARD.** You do, do you? *(after a momentary pause)* I've led a rather adventurous life. I've got into the habit of taking a revolver about with me. I've been in a bit of a jam once or twice. *(smiles)* It's a pleasant feeling to have a gun handy. *(to* **BLORE***)* Don't you agree?

*(Enter* **ARMSTRONG** *left 1; stands down left)*

**BLORE.** We don't carry them. Now, then, I want the truth about this gun –

**LOMBARD.** What a damned suspicious fellow you are, Blore!

**BLORE.** I know a fishy story when I hear one.

**ARMSTRONG.** If it's about that revolver, I'd like to hear what you've got to say.

**LOMBARD.** *(crossing down left)* Oh, well, I got a letter, asking me to come here as the guest of Mr. and Mrs. Owen – It would be worth my while. The writer said that he had heard I'd got a reputation for being a good man in a tight place. There might be some danger, but I'd be all right if I kept my eyes open.

**BLORE.** I'd never have fallen for that.

**LOMBARD.** Well, I did. I was bored. God, how I was bored back in this tame country. It was an intriguing proposition, you must admit.

**BLORE.** Too vague for my liking.

**LOMBARD.** That was the whole charm. It aroused my curiosity.

**BLORE.** Curiosity killed the cat.

**LOMBARD.** *(smiling)* Yes, quite.

**VERA.** Oh, do go and change, please!

**LOMBARD.** I'm going, my sweet, I'm going. The maternal instinct I think it's called.

**VERA.** Don't be ridiculous –

*(***VERA***, up left, collects* **EMILY***'s cup; goes down right with it.* **LOMBARD** *exits left 1.)*

**BLORE.** *(crosses down left)* That's a tall story. If it's true, why didn't he tell it to us last night?

**ARMSTRONG.** He might have thought that this was exactly the emergency for which he had been prepared.

**VERA.** Perhaps it is.

**ARMSTRONG.** *(crosses right center; puts down cup on tabourer and goes right)* I hardly think so. It was just Mr. Owen's little bit of cheese to get him into the trap with the rest of us. He must have known him well enough to rely on his curiosity.

**BLORE.** If it's true, he's a wrong 'un, that man. I wouldn't trust him a yard.

**VERA.** *(up center)* Are you such a good judge of truth?

*(WARGRAVE enters left 1)*

**ARMSTRONG.** *(with a sudden outburst)* We must get out of here – we must before it is too late. *(He is shaking violently.)*

*(BLORE sits down left.)*

**WARGRAVE.** The one thing we must not do is to give away to nerves. *(crosses right above left sofa)*

**ARMSTRONG.** *(sits on fender)* I'm sorry. *(tries to smile)* Rather a case of "Physician, heal thyself." But I've been overworked lately and run down.

**WARGRAVE.** Sleeping badly?

**ARMSTRONG.** Yes. I keep dreaming – Hospital – operations – A knife at my throat – *(shivers)*

**WARGRAVE.** Real nightmares.

**ARMSTRONG.** Yes. *(curiously)* Do you ever dream you're in court – sentencing a man to death?

**WARGRAVE.** *(sits left sofa; smiling)* Are you by any chance referring to a man called Edward Seton? I can assure you I should not lose any sleep over the death of Edward Seton. A particularly brutal and cold-blooded murderer. The jury liked him. They were inclined to let him off. I could see. However – *(with a quiet ferocity)* I cooked Seton's goose.

*(Everyone gives a little shiver.)*

**BLORE.** Brr! Cold in here, isn't it? *(rises; to center)*

**VERA.** *(up right of window)* I wish Rogers would hurry up.

**BLORE.** Yes, where is Rogers? He's been a long time.

**VERA**. He said he'd got to get some sticks.

**BLORE**. *(struck by the word)* Sticks? Sticks? My God, sticks!

**ARMSTRONG**. My God! *(rises, looking at mantelpiece)*

**BLORE**. Is another one gone? Are there only six?

**ARMSTRONG**. *(bewildered)* There are only five.

**VERA**. Five?

> *(They stare at each other.)*

**WARGRAVE**. Rogers and Lombard? *(rises)*

**VERA**. *(with a cry)* Oh, no, not Philip!

> *(**LOMBARD** enters left 1; meets **BLORE** rushing out left 1, calling "Rogers")*

**LOMBARD**. Where the hell is Blore off to like a madman?

**VERA**. *(running to him at left center)* Oh, Philip, I –

> *(warn curtain)*

**WARGRAVE**. *(up right)* Have you seen Rogers?

**LOMBARD**. No, why should I?

**ARMSTRONG**. Two more soldiers have gone.

**LOMBARD**. Two?

**VERA**. I thought it was you –

> *(**BLORE** enters left 1, looking pretty awful.)*

**ARMSTRONG**. Well, what is it?

**BLORE**. *(only just able to speak, his voice quite unlike itself)* In the – scullery.

**VERA**. Is he – ?

**BLORE**. Oh, yes, he's dead all right

**VERA**. How?

**BLORE**. With an axe. Somebody must have come up behind him whilst he was bent over the wood box.

**VERA**. *(wildly)* "One chopped himself in half – then there were six." *(She begins laughing hysterically.)*

**LOMBARD**. Stop it. Vera – Stop it! *(sits her on left sofa, slaps her face, to the others:)* She'll be all right. What next, boys? Bees? Do they keep bees on the island?

*Phillip instead of vera*

*(They stare at him as if not understanding, he keeps his nonchalant manner up with a trace of effort, down to center.)*

**LOMBARD.** Well that's the next verse, isn't it?

"Six little soldier boys playing with a hive;

A bumble bee stung one, and then there were five."

*(he moves round the room)*

A bumble bee stung one – We all look pretty spry, nothing wrong with any of us. *(His glance rests on* **EMILY.***)* My God, you don't think –

*(He goes slowly over to her, bends down, touches her. He then picks up a hypodermic syringe, and turns to face the others.)*

A hypodermic syringe.

**WARGRAVE.** The modern bee sting.

**VERA.** *(stammering)* While she was sitting there – one of us –

**WARGRAVE.** One of us.

*(They look at each other.)*

**ARMSTRONG.** Which of us?

*(curtain)*

# ACT THREE

## Scene I

*(Some hours later. The curtains are drawn and the room is lit by three candles. WARGRAVE, VERA, BLORE, LOMBARD and ARMSTRONG, who is dirty and unshaven, are sitting in silence. LOMBARD sits chair right center, ARMSTRONG on right sofa, WARGRAVE left sofa, VERA on fender, BLORE down left. From time to time they shoot quick, covert glances at each other. VERA watches ARMSTRONG; BLORE watches LOMBARD; LOMBARD watches WARGRAVE; ARMSTRONG watches BLORE and LOMBARD alternately. WARGRAVE watches each in turn, but most often VERA with a long, speculative glance. There is silence for some few minutes. Then LOMBARD speaks suddenly in a loud, jeering voice that makes them all jump.)*

LOMBARD. "Five little soldier boys sitting in a row, watching each other and waiting for the blow." New version up to date! *(He laughs discordantly.)*

ARMSTRONG. I hardly think this is a moment for facetiousness.

LOMBARD. Have to relieve the gloom. *(rises to above right sofa)* Damn that electric plant running down. Let's play a nice round game. What about inventing one called "Suspicions?" A suspects B., B. suspects C. – and so on. Let's start with Blore. It's not hard to guess whom Blore suspects. It sticks out a mile. I'm your fancy, aren't I, Blore?

BLORE. I wouldn't say no to that.

LOMBARD. *(crosses to left a few steps)* You're quite wrong, you know. Abstract justice isn't my line. If I committed

75

murder, there would have to be something in it for me.

**BLORE.** All I say is that you've acted suspiciously from the start. You've told two different stories. You came here with a revolver. Now you say you've lost it.

**LOMBARD.** I have lost it.

**BLORE.** That's a likely story!

**LOMBARD.** What do you think I've done with it? I suggested myself that you should search me.

**BLORE.** Oh! You haven't got it on you. You're too clever for that. But you know where it is.

**LOMBARD.** You mean I've cached it ready for the next time?

**BLORE.** I shouldn't be surprised.

**LOMBARD.** *(crosses right)* Why don't you use your brains, Blore? If I'd wanted to, I could have shot the lot of you by this time, pop, pop, pop, pop, pop.

**BLORE.** Yes, but that's not the big idea. *(points to rhyme)*

**LOMBARD.** *(sits chair right center)* The crazy touch? My God, man, I'm sane enough!

**BLORE.** The doctor says there are some lunatics you'd never know were lunatics. *(looks around at everyone)* That's true enough, I'd say.

**ARMSTRONG.** *(breaking out)* We – we shouldn't just sit here, doing nothing! There must be something – surely, surely, there is something that we can do? If we lit a bonfire –

**BLORE.** In this weather? *(jerks his head towards window)*

**WARGRAVE.** It is, I am afraid, a question of time and patience. The weather will clear. Then we can do something. Light a bonfire, heliograph, signal.

**ARMSTRONG.** *(rises to up right)* A question of time – time? *(laughs in an unbalanced way)* We can't afford time. We shall all be dead.

**WARGRAVE.** I think the precautions we have now adopted will be adequate.

ARMSTRONG. I tell you – we shall all be dead. All but one – He'll think up something else – he's thinking now – *(sits right sofa again)*

LOMBARD. Poor Louise – what was her name – Clees? Was it nerves that made you do her in, Doctor?

ARMSTRONG. *(almost mechanically)* No, drink. I used to be a heavy drinker. God help me, I was drunk when I operated – quite a simple operation. My hand shaking all over the place – *(buries his face in his hands)* I can remember her now – a big, heavy, countrified woman. And I killed her!

LOMBARD. *(rises; to right above* VERA*)* So I was right – that's how it was?

ARMSTRONG. Sister knew, of course, but she was loyal to me – or to the hospital. I gave up drink – gave it up altogether. I went in for a study of nervous diseases.

WARGRAVE. Very successfully. *(rises; to up center)*

ARMSTRONG. One or two lucky shots. Good results with one or two important women. They talked to their friends. For the last year or two I've been so busy I've hardly known which way to turn. I'd got to the top of the tree.

LOMBARD. Until Mr. Unknown Owen – and down will come cradle and doctor and all.

ARMSTRONG. *(rises)* Will you stop your damnable sneering and joking?

WARGRAVE. *(comes down right between* ARMSTRONG *and* LOMBARD*)* Gentlemen, gentlemen, please. We can't afford to quarrel.

LOMBARD. That's okay by me. I apologize.

ARMSTRONG. It's this terrible inactivity that gets on my nerves. *(sits right sofa)*

WARGRAVE. *(to left sofa; sits)* We are adopting, I feel convinced, the only measures possible. So long as we remain together, all within sight of each other, a repetition of the tragedies that have occurred is – must be – impossible. We have all submitted to a search. Therefore, we know that no man is armed either with firearms or a knife. Nor has any man got cyanide or any drug about his person. If we remain, as I say, within sight of each other, nothing can happen.

**ARMSTRONG.** But we can't go on like this – we shall need food – sleep –

**BLORE.** That's what I say.

**WARGRAVE.** Obviously, the murderer's only chance is to get one of us detached from the rest. So long as we prevent that we are safe.

**ARMSTRONG.** Safe – ?

**LOMBARD.** You're very silent, Vera?

**VERA.** There isn't anything to say –

*(pause, **WARGRAVE** rises; to up center)*

I wonder what the time is. It's this awful waiting – waiting for the hours to go by and yet feeling that they may be the last. What is the time?

**LOMBARD.** Half past eight.

**VERA.** Is that all?

**LOMBARD.** Pretty awful light, this. How are the candles holding out?

**BLORE.** There's a whole packet. Storm's dying down a bit, what do you think, sir? *(rises; goes up to window)*

**WARGRAVE.** Perhaps. We mustn't be too optimistic.

**ARMSTRONG.** The murderer's got everything on his side. Even the weather seems to be falling in with his plans.

*(**WARGRAVE** sits left sofa, long pause)*

**BLORE.** *(rising)* What about something to eat?

**VERA.** *(rises, crossing up left)* If you like, I'll go out and open some tongue and make some coffee. But you four stay here. *(to **WARGRAVE**)* That's right, isn't it?

**WARGRAVE.** Not quite. You see, Miss Claythorne, it might be inadvisable to eat or drink something that you had prepared out of our sight.

**VERA**. Oh! *(slowly)* You don't like me, do you?

**WARGRAVE**. It's not a question of likes or dislikes.

*(VERA sits down left.)*

**LOMBARD**. There are very few tricks that will get past you, Sir Lawrence. You know, if you won't be offended at my saying so, you're my fancy.

**WARGRAVE**. *(rises to left, looking at him coldly through his spectacles in the best court manner)* This is hardly the moment, Captain Lombard, for any of us to indulge in the luxury of taking offense.

**LOMBARD**. *(up right center)* I don't think it's Blore. *(to **BLORE**)* I may be wrong, but I can't feel you've got enough imagination for this job. All I can say is if you are the criminal. I take my hat off to you for a damned fine actor.

**BLORE**. Thank you, for nothing. *(sits left sofa)*

**LOMBARD**. *(pause, looks at **ARMSTRONG**)* I don't think it's the Doctor. I don't believe he's got the nerve. *(looks at **VERA** down left)* You've got plenty of nerve. Vera. On the other hand, you strike me as eminently sane. Therefore, you'd only do murder if you had a thoroughly good motive.

**VERA**. *(sarcastically)* Thank you

**ARMSTRONG**. *(rises)* I've thought of something.

**LOMBARD**. Splendid. Animal, vegetable or mineral?

**ARMSTRONG**. That man *(points to **BLORE**)* says he's a police officer. But we've no proof of that. He only said so after the gramophone record, when his name had been given. Before that he was pretending to be a South African millionaire. Perhaps the police officer is another impersonation. What do we know about him? Nothing at all.

**LOMBARD**. He's a policeman all right. Look at his feet.

**BLORE**. *(rises and sits again)* That's enough from you. Mr. Lombard.

*(**ARMSTRONG** sits in chair right center.)*

**LOMBARD**. Well, now we know where we are. By the way, Miss Claythorne suspects you, Doctor. Oh, yes, she does. Haven't you seen her shoot a dirty look from time to time? It all works out quite prettily. I suspect Sir Lawrence. Blore suspects me. Armstrong suspects Blore. *(to* **WARGRAVE***)* What about you, sir?

**WARGRAVE**. Quiet early in the day, I formed a certain conclusion. It seemed to me that everything that had occurred pointed quite unmistakably to one person. *(pause, looks straight ahead)* I am still of the same opinion. *(above left sofa)*

**VERA**. Which one?

**WARGRAVE**. Well – no, I think it would be inadvisable to mention that person's name at the present time.

**LOMBARD**. Inadvisable in the public interest?

**WARGRAVE**. Exactly.

*(Everyone looks at each other.)*

**BLORE**. What about the food idea?

**ARMSTRONG**. No, no, let's stay here. We're safe here.

**VERA**. I can't say I'm hungry.

**LOMBARD**. I'm not ravenous myself. You can go out and have a guzzle by yourself, Blore.

**BLORE**. Tell you what. Suppose I go and bring in a tin of biscuits? *(rises to left 2 door)*

**LOMBARD**. Good idea.

*(***BLORE*** starts to go.)*

Oh, Blore.

**BLORE**. Eh?

**LOMBARD**. An unopened tin, Blore.

*(***BLORE*** goes out and takes candle from bookcase. A pause. Everybody watches the door. A gust of wind. The curtains rattle. ***VERA*** rises. ***WARGRAVE*** sits left sofa.)*

**LOMBARD**. It's only the wind – making the curtains rattle.

**VERA.** *(up center)* I wonder what happened to the bathroom curtain? The one that Rogers missed.

**LOMBARD.** By the wildest stretch of imagination, I cannot see what any homicidal maniac wants with a scarlet oilsilk curtain.

**VERA.** Things seem to have been disappearing. Miss Brent lost a skein of knitting wool.

**LOMBARD.** So the murderer, whoever he or she is, is a kleptomaniac too.

**VERA.** How does it go? "Five little soldier boys – "

**LOMBARD.** "Going in for law, One got in Chancery – "

**VERA.** In chancery, but how could that apply? Unless, of course – *(She looks at* **WARGRAVE.***)*

**WARGRAVE.** Precisely, my dear young lady. That's why I'm sitting right here.

**LOMBARD.** Ah! But I'm casting you for the role of murderer – not victim.

**WARGRAVE.** The term can apply to a boxer.

**LOMBARD.** *(to* **VERA***)* Maybe we'll start a free fight. That seems to let you out, my dear.

**VERA.** That awful rhyme. It keeps going round and round in my head. I think I'll remember it till I die. *(She realizes what she has said and looks around at the others. Pause.)* Mr. Blore's a long time.

**LOMBARD.** I expect the big bad wolf has got him.

**WARGRAVE.** I have asked you once before to try and restrain your rather peculiar sense of humor, Captain Lombard.

**LOMBARD.** Sorry, sir. It must be a form of nervousness.

*(**BLORE** enters left 2 with a tin of biscuits, **VERA** to behind chair right center, **WARGRAVE** rises to left center, takes tin and opens it.)*

**WARGRAVE.** Put your hands up. Search him.

*(**ARMSTRONG** and **LOMBARD** cross to left center; search **BLORE**. **ARMSTRONG** offers biscuits to **VERA**.)*

**VERA**. *(sits right center)* No, thank you.

> (**BLORE** *sits down left.* )

**LOMBARD**. Come now – you've had no dinner. *(to above* **VERA**, *right center)*

**VERA**. I couldn't eat anything.

**LOMBARD**. I warn you – Blore will wolf the lot.

**BLORE**. I don't see why you need be so funny about it. Starving ourselves won't do us any good. *(sadly)* How are we off for cigarettes?

**LOMBARD**. *(takes out his case and opens it; sighs ruefully)* I haven't got any.

**ARMSTRONG**. I've run out too.

**WARGRAVE**. Fortunately, I'm a pipe smoker.

**VERA**. *(rousing herself, crossing down left)* I've got a whole box upstairs in my suitcase. I'll get them. I could do with a cigarette myself. *(pauses at door)* See that you all stay where you are. *(goes out left 1 carrying a candle from bookcase)*

> (**WARGRAVE** *to door, looking after her, leaving tin on sofa)*

**BLORE**. *(rises; fetches tin from sofa – eating solidly, up left center)* Not bad, these biscuits.

**LOMBARD**. What are they, cheese?

**BLORE**. Cheese and celery.

**LOMBARD**. That girl ought to have had some. *(to left)*

**ARMSTRONG**. Her nerves are in a bad state.

**WARGRAVE**. *(to above left sofa)* I don't know that I'd agree with you there. Doctor. Miss Claythorne strikes me as a very cool and resourceful young lady – quite remarkably so.

**LOMBARD**. *(up left center – looking curiously at* **WARGRAVE**) So that's your idea, is it? That she's the guilty party?

**ARMSTRONG**. Hardly likely – a woman!

**WARGRAVE.** You and I, Doctor, see women from slightly different angles.

**BLORE.** *(crosses down right)* What does anyone say to a spot of whiskey?

**LOMBARD.** Good idea, providing we tackle an unopened bottle.

*(An appalling and blood-curdling shriek of utter terror comes from overhead and a heavy thud. All four men start up. LOMBARD and BLORE catch up candles. BLORE takes candle from mantelpiece. All four rush to door left 1 and out in this order: LOMBARD. BLORE, ARMSTRONG and WARGRAVE – the latter is slow getting under way, owing to age. Stage is quite dark as soon as LOMBARD and BLORE have gone through door and before WARGRAVE reaches door. Confused noises off, then, on stage, WARGRAVE's voice calls out, "Who's that?" Sound of a shot. A confused moving about on the stage; voices off also: off faint – then come nearer. Left 2 door opens, then door left 1. BLORE heard swearing off, also ARMSTRONG's voice.)*

**VERA.** *(coming in left 2, stumbling about)* Philip, Philip, where are you? I've lost you.

**LOMBARD.** *(coming in left 1)* Here I am.

**VERA.** Why can't we have some light? It's awful in the dark. You don't know where you are. You don't know where anyone is. *(sits left sofa)*

**LOMBARD.** It's that damned draught on the stairs – blowing all candles out. Here, I've got a lighter. *(lights his and her candle, sits left sofa)*

**VERA.** Where's Doctor Armstrong?

**ARMSTRONG.** *(from hall)* I'm hunting for the matches.

**LOMBARD.** Never mind matches – get some more candles.

**VERA.** I was horrified to death – It went right around my throat –

**LOMBARD.** What did?

**VERA**. The window was open in my room. It blew out the candle as I opened the door. And then a long strand of seaweed touched my throat. I thought, in the dark, that I was being strangled by a wet hand –

*(murmur off left)*

**LOMBARD**. I don't wonder you yelled.

**VERA**. Who hung the seaweed there?

**LOMBARD**. I don't know. But when I find out, he'll be sorry he was ever born.

*(**ARMSTRONG** comes in quietly from left 1.)*

**VERA**. *(sharply)* Who's that?

*(warn curtain)*

**ARMSTRONG**. It's all right, Miss Claythorne. It's only me.

**BLORE**. *(in hall)* Here we are. *(a faint glow through door as he lights candles, comes in carrying candle, crosses right)* Who fired that shot?

*(**VERA** rises; moves left center, turns and screams, light reveals **WARGRAVE** set upright on window seat, red oilsilk curtain draped around shoulders, gray skein of wool plaited into wig on his head, in center of forehead is round dark mark with red trickling from it. Men stand paralyzed, **VERA** screams. **ARMSTRONG** pulls himself together, waves others to stand back and goes over to **WARGRAVE**, bends over him, straightens up.)*

**ARMSTRONG**. He's dead – Shot through the head –

**VERA**. *(leans against window up left)* One got in Chancery – and then there were four

**ARMSTRONG**. Miss Claythorne.

**LOMBARD**. Vera.

**VERA**. You got me out of the way. You got me to go upstairs for cigarettes. You put that seaweed there – You did it all so that you could kill that helpless old man in the dark – you're mad – all of you-crazy. *(Her voice is low and full of horror.)* That's why you wanted the red curtain and the knitting wood – It was all planned – long ago-for that – Oh, my God, let me get out of here –

*(She edges to the left 1 door and rushes out as – )*

*(curtain)*

## Scene II

*(The following morning, it is brilliant sunshine, the room is as it was the night before;* **BLORE**, **LOMBARD** *and* **VERA** *are sitting on the left sofa, backs to the audience, eating tinned tongue on tray.)*

**LOMBARD.** "Three little soldier boys, Sitting in a row, Thinking as they guzzle Who's the next to go?"

**VERA.** Oh, Philip!

**BLORE.** That's all right, Miss Claythorne. I don't minding joking on a full stomach.

**VERA.** I must say I was hungry. But all the same, I don't think I shall ever fancy tinned tongue again.

**BLORE.** I was wanting that meal! I feel a new man.

**LOMBARD.** We'd been nearly twenty-four hours without food. That does lower the morale.

**VERA.** Somehow, in the daylight. everything seems different.

**LOMBARD.** You mustn't forget there's a dangerous homicidal lunatic somewhere loose on this island.

**VERA.** Why is it one doesn't feel jittery about it any more?

**LOMBARD.** Because we know now, beyond any possible doubt, who it is, eh, Blore?

**BLORE.** That's right.

**LOMBARD.** It was the uncertainty before – looking at each other, wondering which.

**VERA.** I said all along it was Doctor Armstrong.

**LOMBARD.** You did, my sweet, you did. Until, of course, you went completely bats and suspected us all.

**VERA.** *(rises to mantelpiece; takes three cigarettes out of box)* It seems rather silly in the light of day.

**LOMBARD.** Very silly.

**BLORE.** Allowing it is Armstrong, what's happened to him?

**LOMBARD.** We know what he wants us to think has happened to him.

**VERA.** *(crosses center, gives* **BLORE** *and* **LOMBARD** *cigarette)* What exactly did you find?

**LOMBARD.** One shoe – just one shoe – sitting prettily on the cliff edge. Inference – Doctor Armstrong has gone completely off his onion and committed suicide.

**BLORE.** *(rises)* All very circumstantial – even to one little china soldier broken over there in the doorway.

**VERA** I think that was rather overdoing it. A man wouldn't think of doing that if he was going to drown himself.

**LOMBARD.** Quite so. But we're fairly sure he didn't drown himself. But he had to make it appear as though he were the seventh victim all according to plan.

**VERA** Suppose he really is dead?

**LOMBARD.** I'm a bit suspicious of death without bodies.

**VERA.** How extraordinary to think that there are five dead bodies in there, and we've been eating tinned tongue.

**LOMBARD.** The delightful feminine disregard for the facts – there are six dead bodies and they are not all in there.

**BLORE.** Oh, no, no. She's right. There are only five.

**LOMBARD.** What about Mrs. Rogers?

**BLORE.** I've counted her. She makes the fifth.

**LOMBARD.** *(rises, a little exasperated)* Now look here: Marston, one. Mrs. Rogers, two. General MacKenzie, three. Rogers, four. Emily Brent, five, and Wargrave, six.

*(VERA takes tray to table up left.)*

**BLORE.** *(counting themselves)* Seven, eight, nine – Armstrong, ten. That's right, old man. Sorry. *(sits left sofa)*

**LOMBARD.** *(sits left sofa)* Don't you think it would be an idea if we brought Mrs. Rogers downstairs and shoved her in the morgue, too?

**BLORE.** I'm a detective, not an undertaker.

**VERA.** *(sits chair right center)* For Heaven's sake, stop talking about bodies. The point is Armstrong murdered them.

**LOMBARD.** We ought to have realized it was Armstrong straight away.

**BLORE.** How do you think Armstrong got hold of your revolver?

**LOMBARD.** Haven't the slightest idea.

**VERA.** Tell me exactly, what happened in the night?

**BLORE.** Well, after you threw a fit of hysterics and locked yourself in your room, we all thought we'd better go to bed. So we all went to bed – and locked ourselves in our rooms.

**LOMBARD.** About an hour later, I heard someone pass my door. I came out and tapped on Blore's door. He was there all right. Then I went to Armstrong's room. It was empty. That's when I tapped on your door and told you to sit tight – whatever happened. Then I came down here. The window on the balcony was open – and my revolver was lying just beside it.

*[handwritten margin note: Blore heard instead of Lombard in Book]*

*[handwritten margin note: Book he finds it in his bedside table]*

**BLORE.** But why the devil should Armstrong chuck that revolver away?

**LOMBARD.** Don't ask me – either an accident or he's crazy.

**VERA.** Where do you think he is?

**LOMBARD.** Lurking somewhere, waiting to have a crack at one of us.

**VERA.** We ought to search the house.

**BLORE.** What – and walk into an ambush?

**VERA.** *(rises)* Oh – I never thought of that.

**LOMBARD.** Are you quite sure you heard no one moving about after we went out?

**VERA.** *(above right sofa)* On, I imagined all sorts of things – but nothing short of setting the house on fire would have got me to unlock my door.

**LOMBARD.** I see – just thoroughly suspicious.

**BLORE.** *(rises to right)* What's the use of talking? What are we going to do?

**LOMBARD.** If you ask me – do nothing. Sit tight and take no risks.

**BLORE.** Look here, I want to go after that fellow.

**LOMBARD.** What a dog of the bulldog breed you are, Blore. By the way, between friends and without prejudice, you did go in for that little spot of perjury, didn't you?

*(VERA sits left end right sofa.)*

**BLORE.** *(sits right center, hesitating)* Well, I don't suppose it makes any odds now. Lendor was innocent, all right. The gang squared me and between us we put him away for a stretch. Mind you, I wouldn't admit it now if it wasn't that –

**LOMBARD.** You think we're all in the same boat?

**BLORE.** Well, I couldn't admit it in front of Mr. Justice Wargrave, could I?

**LOMBARD.** No, hardly.

**BLORE.** *(rises)* I say, that fellow Seton, do you think he was innocent?

**LOMBARD.** I'm quite sure of it. Wargrave had a reason for wanting him out of the way. Well, Blore, I'm delighted you've come off your virtuous perch. I hope you made a tidy bit out of it?

**BLORE.** *(injured)* Nothing like what I ought to have done. They're a mean lot, that Benny gang. I got my promotion, though.

**LOMBARD.** And Lendor got penal servitude and died in gaol.

**BLORE.** I couldn't tell he was going to die, could I?

**LOMBARD.** No, that was your bad luck.

**BLORE.** His, you mean.

**LOMBARD.** Yours, too. Because as a result of that fact you may get your life cut short unpleasantly soon.

**BLORE.** What? Me? By Armstrong? I'll watch it.

**LOMBARD.** You'll have to. Remember there are only three soldier boys there.

**BLORE.** Well, what about you?

**LOMBARD.** I shall be quite all right, thank you. I've been in tight places before and I've got out of them. And I mean to get out of this one. *(pause)* Besides, I've got a revolver.

**BLORE.** *(right end right sofa)* Yes – that revolver. Now listen. You said you found it lying down there. What's to prove you haven't had it all the time?

**LOMBARD.** Same old gramophone record! No room in your head for more than one idea at a time, is there?

**BLORE.** No, but it's a good idea.

**LOMBARD.** And you're sticking to it.

**BLORE.** And I would have thought up a better story than that, if I were you.

**LOMBARD.** I only wanted something simple that a policeman could understand.

**BLORE.** What's wrong with the police?

**LOMBARD.** Nothing – now that you've left the force.

**BLORE.** *(above right sofa)* Now look here, Captain Lombard, if you're an honest man, as you pretend –

**LOMBARD.** Oh, come, Blore, we're neither of us honest.

**BLORE.** If you're telling the truth for once, you ought to do the square thing and chuck that revolver down there.

**LOMBARD.** Don't be an ass.

**BLORE.** I've said I'll go through the house looking for Armstrong, haven't I? If I'm willing to do that, will you lend me that revolver?

**LOMBARD.** *(rises to down center)* No, I won't. That revolver's mine. It's my revolver and I'm sticking to it.

**BLORE.** *(angrily)* Then do you know what I'm beginning to think?

**LOMBARD.** You're not beginning to think it, you square-headed flattie. You thought it last night, and now you've gone back to your original idea. I'm the one and only U.N. Unknown Owen. Is that it?

**BLORE.** I won't contradict you.

LOMBARD. Well, think what you damned well please. But I warn you –

VERA. *(incisively)* I think you are both behaving like a pair of children.

*(They both look at her rather sheepishly.)*

LOMBARD. Sorry, teacher.

VERA. *(to* BLORE, *scornfully)* Of course, Captain Lombard isn't the unknown. The Unknown Owen is Armstrong – and I'll tell you one very good proof of it.

BLORE. Oh, what?

VERA. Think of the rhyme. "Four little soldier boys – going out to sea. A red herring swallowed one, and then there were three." Don't you see the subtlety of it? A red herring? That's Armstrong's pretended suicide, but it's only a red herring – so really he isn't dead!

BLORE. That's very ingenious.

VERA. To my mind, it's absolute proof. You see, it's all mad because he's mad. He takes a queer, childish, crazy pleasure in sticking to the rhyme and making everything happen in that way. Dressing up the Judge, killing Rogers when he was chopping sticks; using a hypodermic needle on Miss Brent, when he might just as well have drugged her. He's got to make it all fit in.

BLORE. And that might give us a pointer. Where do we go from here? *(goes up to mantelpiece and reads:)*
"Three little soldier boys walking in the zoo.
A big bear hugged one and then there were two."
*(He laughs.)*
He'll have a job with that one. There's no zoo on this island!

*(His laugh is cut short as he sees the big bear rug on which he is standing. He edges off the rug and turns to* LOMBARD.*)*

I say, Captain Lombard, what about a nice bottle of beer?

**LOMBARD.** Do stop thinking about your stomach, Blore. This craving for food and drink will be your undoing.

**BLORE.** But there's plenty of beer in the kitchen.

**LOMBARD.** Yes, and if anyone wanted to get rid of you, the first place they'd think putting a lethal dose would be in a nice bottle of beer.

*(From outside comes the sound of a motorboat hooter.)*

**BLORE.** What's that? A boat! A boat!

*(**ALL** rush to balcony to left. **BLORE** rushes out onto balcony, there is a scream, then a crash and thud.)*

**VERA.** Oh, God! *(puts hands over eyes)*

*(**LOMBARD**, revolver in hand, rushes to window, looks out, then returns slowly to room. **VERA** sits down left.)*

**LOMBARD.** Blore's got his.

**VERA.** How?

**LOMBARD.** A booby trap – all set – a wire across the door attached to something above.

**VERA.** Is he?

**LOMBARD.** Yes. Crushed. Head stove in. That great bronze bear holding a clock, from the landing.

**VERA.** A bear? Oh, how ghastly! It's this awful childishness!

**LOMBARD.** I know. God, what a fool Blore was!

**VERA.** And now there are two.

**LOMBARD.** *(to down left)* Yes, and we'll have to be very careful of ourselves.

**VERA.** We shan't do it. He'll get us. We'll never get away from this island!

**LOMBARD.** Oh, yes, we will, I've never been beaten yet.

**VERA.** Don't you feel – that there's someone – now – in this room – watching us, watching and waiting?

**LOMBARD.** That's just nerves.

**VERA.** Then you do feel it?

**LOMBARD.** *(fiercely)* No, I don't.

**VERA.** *(rises, to center)* Please, Philip, let's get out of this house – anywhere. Perhaps if that was a boat, they'll see us.

LOMBARD. All right. We'll go to the top of the island and wait for relief to come. It's sheer cliff on the far side and we can see if anyone approaches from the house.

VERA. Anything's better than staying here.

LOMBARD. Won't you be rather cold in that dress?

VERA. I'd be colder if I were dead.

LOMBARD. Perhaps you're right. *(goes to window)* A quick reconnaissance.

VERA. Be careful, Philip – please! *(follows him to window)*

LOMBARD. I'm not Blore. There's no window directly above. *(He goes out on balcony and looks down. He is arrested by what he sees.)* Hullo, there's something washed up on the rocks.

VERA. What? *(she joins him)* It looks like a body.

LOMBARD. *(in a strange new voice)* You'd better wait in there. I'm going to have a look.

*(He exits to left on Balcony, VERA back into room; her face is full of conflicting emotions.)*

VERA. Armstrong – Armstrong's body –

LOMBARD. *(comes in very slowly)* It's Armstrong drowned – washed up at high water mark.

VERA. So there's no one on the island – no one at all except us two.

LOMBARD. Yes, Vera. Now we know where we are.

VERA. Now we know where we are?

LOMBARD. A very pretty trick of yours, with that wire. Quite neat. Old Wargrave always knew you were dangerous.

VERA. You –

LOMBARD. So you did drown that kid after all.

VERA. I didn't! That's where you're wrong. Please believe me. Please listen to me!

LOMBARD. *(crossing down left)* I'm listening. You'd better make it a good story.

**VERA.** *(above right sofa)* It's isn't a story. It's the truth. I didn't kill that child. It was someone else.

**LOMBARD.** Who?

**VERA.** A man. Peter's uncle. I was in love with him.

**LOMBARD.** This is getting quite interesting.

**VERA.** Don't sneer. It was hell. Absolute hell. Peter was born after his father's death. If he'd been a girl, Hugh would have got everything.

**LOMBARD.** Well-known tale of the wicked uncle.

**VERA.** Yes – he was wicked – and I didn't know. He said he loved me, but that he was too poor to marry. There was a rock far out that Peter was always wanting to swim to. Of course, I wouldn't let him. It was dangerous. One day we were on the beach and I had to go back to the house for something I'd forgotten. When I got back to the rock, I looked down and saw Peter swimming out to the rock. I knew he hadn't a chance, the current had got him already. I flew towards the beach and Hugh tried to stop me. "Don't be a fool," he said. "I told the little ass he could do it."

**LOMBARD.** Go on. This is interesting.

**VERA.** I pushed past him – he tried to stop me, but I got away and rushed down. I plunged into the sea and swam after Peter. He'd gone before I could get to him.

**LOMBARD.** And everything went off well at the inquest. They called you a plucky girl, and you kept discreetly quiet about Hugh's part in the business.

**VERA.** Do you think anyone would have believed me? Besides, I couldn't! I really was in love with him.

**LOMBARD.** Well, it's a pretty story. And then I suppose Hugh let you down?

**VERA.** Do you think I ever wanted to see him again?

**LOMBARD.** You certainly are an accomplished liar, Vera.

**VERA.** Can't you believe the truth when you hear it?

**LOMBARD.** Who set the trap that killed Blore? I didn't – and Armstrong's dead. I've broken most of the

*They don't die because they are innocent*

Commandments in my time – and I'm no saint. But there's one thing I won't stand for and that's murder.

**VERA.** You won't stand for murder. What about those natives you left to die in Africa?

**LOMBARD.** That's what's so damn funny – I didn't.

**VERA.** What do you mean?

**LOMBARD.** For once – just once, mark you, I played the hero. Risked my life to save the lives of my men, left them my rifle and ammunition and all the food there was – and took a chance through the bush. By the most incredible luck it came off – but it wasn't in time to save them. And the rumor got around that I'd deliberately abandoned my men. There's life for you!

**VERA.** Do you expect me to believe that? Why, you actually admitted the whole thing.

**LOMBARD.** I know. I got such a kick out of watching their faces.

**VERA.** You can't fool me with a stupid lie like that.

**LOMBARD.** *(completely losing his temper)* Blast you!

*Does happen*

**VERA.** *(to right window)* Why didn't I see it before? It's there in your face – the face of a killer –

**LOMBARD.** You can't fool me any longer.

**VERA.** Oh –

*(VERA sways forward as if fainting. LOMBARD runs to catch her. She wrests the revolver from him.)*

Now!

**LOMBARD.** *(backing away down left)* You cunning little devil!

**VERA.** If you come one step nearer, I'll shoot.

**LOMBARD.** You – young, lovely, and quite, quite mad.

*(LOMBARD makes a movement to VERA, she shoots, he falls down left. She goes over to him, her eyes full of horror as she realizes what she has done. The revolver falls from her hand. Suddenly she hears a low laugh coming from the study door. She turns her head slowly in*

*Phil is innocent*

*that direction. The laughter grows louder, the right door slowly opens and* **WARGRAVE** *enters. He carries a rope in his hand.)*

**WARGRAVE.** It's all come true. My Ten Little Soldiers plan – My rhyme – my rhyme –

**VERA.** Ah! *(stifled scream)*

**WARGRAVE.** *(angrily)* Silence in Court! *(looks around suspiciously)* If there is any more noise, I shall have the Court cleared. *(down right center)* It's all right, my dear. It's all right. Don't be frightened. This is a Court of Justice. You'll get justice here.

*(crosses left, locks doors left 2 and left 1;* **VERA** *to right, confidentially)*

You thought I was a ghost. You thought I was dead. *(above right sofa)* Armstrong said I was dead. That was the clever part of my plan. Said we'd trap the murderer. We'd fix up my supposed death so I should be free to spy upon the guilty one. He thought it an excellent plan – came out that night to meet me by the cliff without any suspicion. I sent him over with a push – so easily. He swallowed my red herring all right.

*(***VERA*** is petrified with horror, in a confidential manner.)*

You know, Vera Claythorne, all my life I've wanted to take life – yes, to take life. I've had to get what enjoyment I could out of sentencing the guilty to death.

*(***VERA*** moves to the revolver.)*

I always enjoyed that – but it wasn't enough. I wanted more – I wanted to do it myself with my own hands –

*(***WARGRAVE*** follows* **VERA** *to left,* **VERA** *leans against left 1 door, suddenly curbs excitement and speaks with severe dignity.)*

But I'm a Judge of the High Court. I've got a sense of justice. *(as if listening to an echo)* As between our Sovereign Lord the King and the prisoner at the Bar

– will true deliverance make – Guilty, my Lord. Yes. *(nods head)* Guilty. You were all guilty, you know, but the Law couldn't touch you, so I had to take the Law into my own hands. *(holds up hands in a frenzy of delight)* Into my own hands! Silence in the Court!

*(VERA hammers on left 1 door. WARGRAVE takes her arm and drags her to right above left sofa.)*

Anthony Marston first. Then Mrs. Rogers. Barbitone in the brandy. MacKenzie – stabbed. Got Rogers with an axe when he was chopping sticks. Doped Emily Brent's coffee so she couldn't feel the hypodermic. Booby trap for Blore. *(confidentially)* Blore was a fool. I always knew it would be easy to get Blore. Returning that revolver was a clever touch. Made the end interesting. I knew you two would suspect each other in the end. The question was, who'd win out? I banked on you, my dear. The female of the species. Besides, it's always more exciting to have a girl at the end.

*(He steps onto sofa, and VERA falls to the ground.)*

Prisoner at the Bar, have you anything to say why sentence should not be passed on you? Vera Elizabeth Claythorne, I sentence you to death –

*(warn curtain)*

VERA. *(with a sudden outcry)* Stop! Stop! I'm not guilty! I'm not guilty!

WARGRAVE. Ah, they all say that. Must plead not guilty. Unless, of course, you're going all out for a verdict of insanity. But you're not mad. *(very reasonably)* I'm mad, but you're not.

VERA. But I am innocent!! I swear it! I never killed that child. I never wanted to kill him. You're a Judge. You know when a person is guilty and when they're innocent. I swear I'm telling the truth.

WARGRAVE. So you didn't drown that boy after all? Very interesting. But it doesn't matter much now, does it?

**VERA**. What – *(makes inarticulate sounds as the rope swings in front of her)*

**WARGRAVE**. I can't spoil my lovely rhyme. My ten little soldier boys. You're the last one. One little solider boy left all alone. He went and hanged himself. I must have my hanging – my hanging –

*(***LOMBARD*** *comes slowly to, picks up revolver and shoots.* **WARGRAVE** *falls back off the sofa.)*

**VERA**. Philip – Philip –

*(They both sit on floor in front of sofa.)*

**LOMBARD**. It's all right, darling. It's all right.

**VERA**. I thought you were dead. I thought I'd killed you.

**LOMBARD**. Thank God, women can't shoot straight. At least, not straight enough.

**VERA**. I shall never forget this.

**LOMBARD**. Oh, yes, you will. You know there's another ending to that Ten Little Soldier Boys rhyme:
"One little soldier boy, left all alone,
We got married – and then there were none!"

*(He takes the rope and puts his head in noose too. He kisses her. There is the sound of a motor hooter.)*

### END OF THE PLAY

# PROPERTY PLOT

2 sofas

1 wing armchair

1 club armchair

1 round-back easy chair

1 narrow bookcase filled with books

2 20-inch end tables

1 oval standard-size table

1 18-inch round table

1 upholstered 4-foot bench

1 18-inch tabouret

1 antique chest of drawers

1 wicker armchair *(outside of center door)*

1 mantelpiece

1 large frame containing the 'Ten Little Soldier Boys" rhymes *(hanging over mantel)*

10 china soldier boys *(clustered on mantel)*

5 cigarette boxes

5 ash trays

2 32-cal. revolvers and blank cartridges

3 3-light candlesticks with candles

Matches *(on tables, mantel, chest, bookcase)*

Cigarettes

1 silver tray

1 metal tray

1 bearskin

1 andiron set

1 fireplace screen

1 small sofa

2 bronze statutes

1 blue carpet *(for steps)*

1 6 x 10-foot carpet

1 7 x 4 1/2-foot carpet

1 6 x 3 1/2-foot carpet

Thunder, wind and rain effects

1 scarf for buffet

1 doctor's bag

6 pieces of luggage, including one lady's overnight bag

1 market basket containing filled bags

1 old-fashioned clock *(for top of bookcase)*

1 pair of decanters, filled

2 dozen highball glasses

1 glass pitcher of water

1 bottle of White Rock

1 bottle opener

1 white face towel
2 urns of green foliage
1 water glass
1 brandy glass
1 short highball glass
1 hurricane lamp lit with candle
1 English shooting stick
Smelling salts
1 bunch of trunk keys
1 silver tray containing a 3-piece china coffee set filled with Coca-Cola, 6
    demitasse cups and saucers, small spoons and napkins
2 cushions for sofas
1 pair of tortoise shell glasses
Draperies for all windows
Ivy foliage *(on stone wall outside windows)*
1 hypodermic needle
1 noose to slide
1 cocktail shaker
1 Bible
1 knitting bag
1 pair steel knitting needles
6 men's handkerchiefs
1 spring camelhair coat and hat
1 shoulder holster
1 Dunhill cigarette lighter
1 sprinkling can *(to wet raincoats offstage)*
1 water cloth
1 pull cord *(on wall)*
2 counterweights *(for effect of body falling)*
1 hangman's rope *(noose)*
1 vase of flowers
1 6-foot piece of plant
2 pieces of metal *(to drop to floor for effect)*

# SET DESIGN

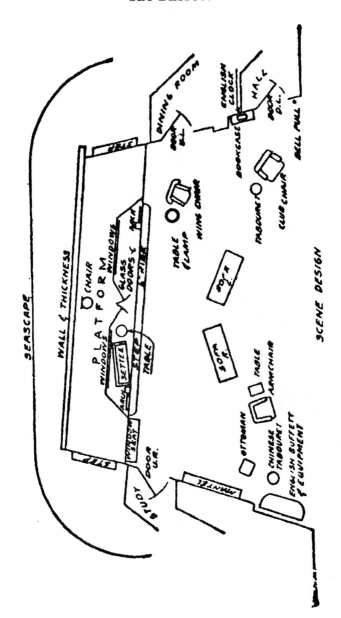